Other Books by Harriet Steel

Becoming Lola

Salvation

City of Dreams

Following the Dream

The Inspector de Silva Mysteries:

Trouble in Nuala

Dark Clouds over Nuala

AN INSPECTOR DE SILVA MYSTERY

OFFSTAGE IN NUALA

HARRIET STEEL

First published 2017

Author's Note and Acknowledgements

Welcome to the third book in my Inspector de Silva mystery series. Like the earlier ones, this is a self-contained story but, wearing my reader's hat, I usually find that my enjoyment of a series is deepened by reading the books in order and getting to know major characters well. With that in mind, I have included thumbnail sketches of those featuring here who took a major part in previous stories. I have also reprinted the introduction, with apologies to those who have already read it.

Two years ago, I had the great good fortune to visit the island of Sri Lanka, the former Ceylon. I fell in love with the country straight away, awed by its tremendous natural beauty and the charm and friendliness of its people who seem to have recovered extraordinarily well from the tragic civil war between the two main ethnic groups, the Sinhalese and the Tamils. I had been planning to write a new detective series for some time and when I came home, I decided to set it in Ceylon in the 1930s, a time when British Colonial rule created interesting contrasts, and sometimes conflicts, with traditional culture. Thus, Inspector Shanti de Silva and his friends were born.

I owe many thanks to everyone who helped with this book. My editor, John Hudspith, was, as usual, invaluable and Jane Dixon Smith designed my favourite cover yet as well as the elegant layout. Praise from the many readers who told me that they enjoyed the two previous books in this series and wanted to know what Inspector de Silva and his friends got up to next encouraged me to keep going. Above all, heartfelt thanks go to my husband, Roger, without whose unfailing encouragement and support I might never have reached the end.

All characters in the book are fictitious with the exception of well-known historical figures. Nuala is also fictitious although loosely based on the town of Nuwara Eliya. Any mistakes are my own.

**Characters who appear regularly
in the Inspector de Silva Mysteries**

Inspector Shanti de Silva. He began his police career in
Ceylon's capital city, Colombo, but, in middle age, he married and accepted a promotion to inspector in charge of the
small force in the hill town of Nuala. Likes: a quiet life with
his beloved wife; his car; good food; his garden. Dislikes:
interference in his work by his British masters; formal occasions. Race and religion: Sinhalese, Buddhist.

Sergeant Prasanna. In his mid-twenties, recently married,
and doing well in his job. Likes: cricket and is exceptionally
good at it. Race and religion: Sinhalese, Buddhist.

Constable Nadar. A few years younger than Prasanna and
less confident. Married with a baby boy. Likes: his food;
making toys for his baby son. Dislikes: sleepless nights.
Race and religion: Tamil, Hindu.

The British:

Jane de Silva. She came to Ceylon as a governess to a
wealthy colonial family and met and married de Silva a few
years later. A no-nonsense lady with a dry sense of humour.
Likes: detective novels, cinema, and dancing. Dislikes:
snobbishness.

Archie Clutterbuck. Assistant government agent in Nuala
and as such, responsible for administration and keeping law
and order in the area. Likes: his Labrador, Darcy; fishing;

hunting big game. Dislikes: being argued with; the heat.

Florence Clutterbuck. Archie's wife, a stout, forthright lady. Likes: being queen bee; organising other people. Dislikes: people who don't defer to her at all times.

William Petrie. Government agent for the Central Province and therefore Archie Clutterbuck's boss. A charming exterior hides a steely character. Likes: getting things done. Dislikes: inefficiency.

Doctor David Hebden. Doctor for the Nuala area. He travelled widely before ending up in Nuala. Unmarried and hitherto, under his professional shell, rather shy. Likes: cricket. Dislikes: formality.

CHAPTER 1

Late November 1936

Nuala's Gaiety Theatre had never decided whether it wanted to be in the style of a Roman temple or a medieval castle. On its busy roof, columned classical domes rubbed shoulders with crenelated turrets in an architectural argument that was only partially settled by the simpler decoration of the walls below. There, whitewashed plaster was set off by the stone trim of the windows and the triple bank of entrance doors. Without a doubt, thought Inspector de Silva, the effect of the lower half of the building was the more restful of the two.

With Jane on his arm, he joined the crowd that mounted the stairs. At the top of the steep flight, ushers in red and gold livery stood on either side of the main door, bowing to the theatregoers passing through. 'Goodness,' murmured Jane. 'I hadn't expected it to be such a smart occasion. I'm afraid I'm rather underdressed.' She looked down at her blue cotton frock and its matching woollen stole with a frown.

'Nonsense, you look perfect.'

'It's kind of you to say so, dear, but I can't help feeling I should have worn something more formal. I suppose it's so long since a professional theatre company's come to Nuala that the place has been all spruced up and people have made a special effort too.'

He squeezed her hand. 'But it won't make them enjoy the play any more than we shall.'

Jane smiled. 'I don't think that's the point, dear.'

De Silva shrugged. He wasn't keen on the British habit of wearing formal dress. It seemed especially unwarranted when you were going to spend most of the evening in darkness watching a play. As he was not on duty, he had come dressed for comfort in traditional loose white trousers and long tunic.

Inside, chatter and laughter filled the foyer and, despite the many large fans suspended from the gilded ceiling, the heat was overpowering.

'There are the Clutterbucks,' said Jane. 'Oh dear, Florence really has dressed up.'

The assistant government agent's wife's ample figure was encased in shiny, emerald-green satin and festooned with pearls. She glimpsed the de Silvas through the crowd and bestowed a wave.

'And has managed to resemble one of your British Christmas trees,' de Silva whispered.

Jane's lips twitched. 'Shanti! Really! I hope she doesn't realise what you're saying.'

'I don't expect so. Florence may be very good at ferreting things out, but I doubt she can lip read.'

'Look, there's Doctor Hebden coming to talk to them. What a shame he's on his own.'

De Silva raised an eyebrow. 'Don't tell me you're still trying to marry him off?'

'Is there anything wrong with that? I like Doctor Hebden and I think it's time he had a wife.'

'I suppose I can't argue with you there.' De Silva grinned. 'I've no complaints about the married state.'

'I should hope not.'

Archie Clutterbuck saw them and beckoned. They made their way through the crowd to join the little group.

'Evening, de Silva. And Mrs de Silva. A pleasure to see you, ma'am.'

Clutterbuck bowed to Jane, the buttons on his dinner jacket straining over his rotund middle as he did so. His neck was the colour of rare beefsteak against the white of his starched dress shirt and his forehead glistened. 'Warm in this crowd, eh? I hope it will be cooler inside.'

'I hope so too, sir,' replied de Silva. 'May I say how charming you look, Mrs Clutterbuck?'

Florence simpered. 'Why thank you, Inspector. I thought one ought to make an effort when the Danforths have honoured us with a visit. Alexander Danforth and his wife have appeared in the West End, you know.'

'So Jane tells me, ma'am. We have both been eagerly anticipating this evening. The programme looks most interesting.'

'Ah, dear Mr Shakespeare,' Florence gushed, laying the palm of her hand on her bosom. De Silva suppressed a chuckle. From the way she was behaving, it was as if she was under some delusion she had known the playwright in a previous life. 'Such sublime language,' she went on. 'I do hope it won't be too hard for you to follow, Inspector.'

De Silva smiled politely. 'I shall do my best, ma'am. With Jane's help, I have been doing a little homework to that end.'

'Very laudable,' Archie cut in. 'Interested to hear what you make of it. I must say, defeats me a lot of the time. Never get the jokes.'

Florence shot him one of her looks.

A bell sounded. 'Time we were taking our seats, I think,' said Archie in a voice tinged with reluctance.

'You mustn't mind Florence,' Jane whispered as they fell into step behind the Clutterbucks. 'You know how she loves to polish her literary credentials.'

'I do know, and I won't let it worry me.'

Inside the auditorium, they were greeted by a more coherent scheme of decoration than the outside of the theatre presented, with red-plush seats and cream walls embellished with gilded detail. Golden cupids cavorted across the front of the dress circle. De Silva saw the Clutterbucks take their places in a box to one side of the stage; he half expected Florence to whip out a lorgnette and start surveying the audience below her with a critical eye.

Looking round, he wondered what Shakespeare would have made of the elegant setting. From what he'd learnt, the famous bard had been used to very different surroundings. Theatres in his day had, apparently, been built of wood, largely open to the elements, and they were not reserved for the well off. De Silva imagined the heat of hundreds of people packed into the pit in front of the stage; the shouts and the laughter; the tramp of boots on the wooden stairs as those with more money to spend went up to take their seats in the galleries. Lastly, his acutely sensitive nose wrinkled at the thought of the smell of unwashed bodies. Of necessity, laxer standards of hygiene had applied in those days.

Jane nudged him. 'You're very quiet. Are you're sure you're not cross?'

'What? Oh, you mean Florence. No, not at all. I was just thinking about the theatres Shakespeare would have known.'

It was true Florence didn't trouble him, at least not much. In his dealings with the British, he had long ago discovered that it was best not to be thin-skinned.

The bell rang for a second time.

'Oh dear.' Hurriedly, Jane opened the programme in her lap. 'We haven't looked at this yet and they'll be starting in three minutes.'

De Silva glanced across and saw that the first two pages contained photographs and short biographies of the cast. At the head of the list came Alexander Danforth himself. De

Silva recognised him as the man he had noticed two days previously, driving around town in a silver-grey Lagonda, although the company had originally arrived in Nuala in an elderly bus painted every colour of the rainbow. What with that and the huge piles of luggage strapped precariously to its roof, it was an arresting sight and had caused a great deal of excitement. The names on the stickers affixed to the bus – Cairo, Delhi, Bombay, Calcutta, Singapore and many others were, presumably, places that the company had already visited.

From a distance, in the bazaar, Danforth had looked about forty, powerfully built with springy dark hair and a hawk-like nose. The photograph in the programme must be an old one for it made him look considerably younger than he had in real life. The large, dark eyes, surmounted by luxuriant eyebrows, had a glint of humour in them, but they looked as if they didn't miss much. Overall, de Silva sensed an electric, very masculine presence.

The photograph of Danforth's wife, Kathleen, conveyed a very different impression. She looked into the camera with a dreamy, seductive gaze. If the camera didn't lie, the witchery in those eyes would be enough to make all but the most impervious of men her slaves. The tones of her skin and her heavy mass of hair were muted, as if the photograph had been taken through a veil of the finest gauze.

Jane cleared her throat. 'You don't need to stare for quite so long, dear.'

He chuckled. 'Sorry.'

She turned the page and ran an eye down the cast list. 'Mrs Danforth is playing Queen Gertrude. I wondered if she would take the part of Ophelia but that's being played by someone called Emerald Watson.'

She turned back to the photograph pages and pointed to a picture of a young woman with dark, curly hair and a vivacious face. 'How pretty she is, don't you think?'

'Very pretty,' de Silva agreed.

In contrast to Kathleen Danforth, Emerald Watson leant forward eagerly with her lips curved in a smile. He imagined her as captain of the hockey team at one of those jolly British schools one read about in novels. He suspected she would be livelier company than Mrs Danforth, and considerably less overwhelming.

'The ghost of Hamlet's father is played by a man called Frank Sheridan,' Jane went on. 'Horatio, Hamlet's friend, is played by Paul Mayne.' She pointed to his photograph on the opposite page to the Danforths – a good-looking young man with soulful eyes. 'Polonius is played by Michael Morville, and Laertes—'

'Who's he?'

'Don't you remember? He's Ophelia's brother and Polonius is their father.'

'Ah yes.'

'Laertes is played by Frank Sheridan too.'

'What about the rest of the characters?'

'Oh, I forgot to tell you, some of the members of our own Amateur Dramatic Society are taking part.'

'Hmm. I'm glad I'm not a member.'

She squeezed his arm. 'Nonsense, I'm sure you would do very well.'

'I doubt it.'

The lights dimmed and she closed the programme. 'Oh good, they're beginning.'

Although de Silva had been familiar with some of the well-known lines from Hamlet, he had only recently tackled the complete play. With Jane's help, he had found the plot quite easy to follow, even if a lot of the language was archaic. He wondered if people really talked like that in Shakespeare's day, or whether literary language was more formal and high-flown than the everyday. A pity one would never know.

During the interval, he sipped his lemonade and listened while Florence rhapsodised about the play. As far as he had the experience to tell, the acting was very good, particularly Alexander Danforth's performance in the role of Hamlet. Even though he was rather old for the part, he brought a vigour to it that might be envied by a much younger man, and his sonorous voice was very pleasing to the ear.

'What with Florence gushing on so, I didn't get much chance to ask if you were enjoying the play,' said Jane as they walked to the car at the end of the evening.

He held open the Morris's passenger door and she slid in.

'I was and, I'll admit it now, more than I expected to.' He settled into the driving seat and started the engine. 'Everyone was excellent and they brought the play to life – treachery, vengeance, murder – it reminded me of an average week in the Colombo police force.'

Jane laughed. 'Colombo wasn't that bad, I hope.'

He grinned. 'Not all of the time.'

The Morris left the streets of town behind and purred along the quiet road that led to Sunnybank.

'I thought that the Amateur Dramatic Society's members acquitted themselves admirably,' Jane remarked. 'And they seemed to be really enjoying it.'

'I'm surprised Florence didn't take part. Isn't she one of them?'

'Yes, but only for play readings. Anyway, there were no female parts left for her to play.'

'True.'

They drove on in silence. The Morris's headlamps turned the road into a ribbon of light, darkening the jungle on either side. Even though there was no other traffic, de Silva kept to a slow, steady speed. A flickering shadow beside the road might be a wild animal poised to run across. It was as well to be very cautious when driving at night.

'Certainly, Florence would have looked magnificent dressed in armour as a soldier,' he observed after a few moments. 'The sight would have struck terror into the stoutest heart.'

Jane giggled. 'Shanti, you shouldn't keep poking fun at her. One day, she might find out.'

He reached out and patted her hand. 'But it's so tempting and you know you're just as bad.'

'Poor Florence; she does try very hard with all her causes and activities. It's a pity she has to be so bossy. I'm not sure that Archie enjoyed the evening. I don't think he cares for serious theatre much. But he did tell me once that he liked a good musical. He and Florence seem to have very different tastes, don't they? It makes one wonder if they're really happy together.'

He shrugged. 'People say opposites attract.'

Jane stifled a yawn. 'I suppose they have been married for a long time.'

'So, there you are. There must be affection between them.'

'I like to think so.'

'The scene where the ghost of Hamlet's father comes up from below the stage was suitably eerie,' de Silva said after another short silence. 'I expect the owner of Gopallawa Motors was relieved. He told me he had to send a mechanic up to repair the contraption that moves the section of stage there up and down. He wouldn't like it getting about that his garage does a bad job.'

'I doubt that stage trap's been used for years. I didn't even know the theatre had one. Do you remember the friend I told you about in London? The lady I used to go to the theatre with.'

'Yes.'

'Well, she had a cousin who worked at the Theatre Royal in Drury Lane and he invited us to go behind the scenes once.'

'I imagine that was right up your street.'

'I'm sure you would have found it fascinating too. They had all sorts of clever ways of creating effects. Some of them used hydraulics – water pressure.'

He raised an eyebrow. 'Here in Ceylon, we've understood how to tame water for thousands of years.'

'I'm sorry, dear. I know you have.'

'Thank you,' he said, feeling a little guilty for being tetchy. Perhaps Florence Clutterbuck's remark earlier in the evening had annoyed him more than he liked to admit. 'Go on.'

'Let me see… Oh yes, there was a special trap made of triangular wedges of leather. My friend's cousin called it a star trap. An actor has to stand on a circular platform below it and then be hauled up very fast using counterweights so that, as the trap opens, he shoots into the air at great speed. Apparently, it was very popular in pantomimes when the story called for surprise entrances.'

'It sounds dangerous.'

'Yes, he admitted there were quite a few mishaps.'

The Morris turned into the drive and the gravel crackled under its wheels as they drew up at the front porch. De Silva turned off the engine and applied the handbrake. 'Home at last.'

He got out and came round to Jane's side of the car to open the door for her; she climbed out and planted a kiss on his cheek.

'What was that for?'

'For being so patient with Florence.'

He grimaced. 'If I'm honest, I'm not sure I am.'

'Well, we're home now, so you don't need to be any longer.'

She bent down and picked up a pebble from the drive. 'And if it will make you feel better, you can pretend this is her and throw it into that prickly bush over there.'

'Mm, it's tempting.' He took the pebble and weighed it in one hand before dropping it back on the ground. 'On second thoughts, I think a nightcap might be the better solution.'

'Whisky and soda?'

'What a good idea.'

CHAPTER 2

'Do you have a busy day planned, dear?' asked Jane as they breakfasted a few mornings later.

De Silva raised a forkful of string hoppers to his mouth. The noodles were just as he liked them, steaming hot and coated with fresh curry sauce and fiery coconut relish. 'Not particularly. Why do you ask?'

'I forgot to order some of the spices Cook asked for. If you have time, would you mind going to the bazaar and buying them?'

'Not at all. I'll drop in on my way to the station.'

He found a place to park the Morris just outside the shop Jane favoured and went in. The interior was cool as very little sunshine filtered through its only window. Sacks of dried chillies leant against the wall to the right of the counter and wooden boxes and copper bowls displayed every kind of spice from cumin seeds and coriander pods to turmeric and rose-gold threads of saffron. Powerful aromas tickled de Silva's nose. He handed over Jane's list and chatted to the owner while the spices were weighed out and the packages neatly wrapped with brown paper and twine.

Coming out of the shop, he paused to let his eyes readjust to the brightness of the sun. A moment later, he was glad he had done so; the roar of an engine made him jump and the silver-grey Lagonda swept by a few feet from where he stood. His heartbeat quickened at the narrow escape but he soon recovered and gazed after the car in admiration. It had the elegance of a leopard and, given an open road, it could probably approach the speed.

The Lagonda halted abruptly a little further down the street and the tall figure of Alexander Danforth got out.

Danforth strode back to where de Silva stood. 'My dear sir, my apologies! No harm done, I hope. I was distracted by the beauty of the morning and your charming town. I haven't yet had the pleasure of making your acquaintance, but am I right in thinking I'm addressing Inspector Shanti de Silva?'

There was a lilt to Danforth's voice that de Silva couldn't place. He hadn't noticed it when Danforth was playing Hamlet. Regaining his composure, he smiled. 'You are, sir, and no harm is done.'

'I'm very glad to hear it.'

Danforth held out his hand. 'Alexander Danforth, at your service.'

'You need no introduction, sir,' said de Silva, shaking the proffered hand. 'I'm glad to have the opportunity of telling you how much my wife and I enjoyed the play the other evening.'

'Ah, excellent. I must say, it was something of an occasion for me, it being my one hundredth performance of the part of Hamlet. But I forget my manners; let me introduce you to our Ophelia, Miss Emerald Watson.'

The young woman had climbed out of the car and was walking towards them. De Silva admired her graceful air. Now she was dressed in modern clothing that didn't obscure her figure, he saw that it was very trim. The hair that had been concealed by Ophelia's veil framed her piquant face with a mass of dark curls. Her full lips were rosy and her hazel eyes sparkled.

Danforth held out his hand to her. 'Emerald, my dear, come and meet Inspector de Silva. He's something of a celebrity in these parts, I understand.'

'I'm not sure I can lay claim to that, ma'am.' De Silva made a bow. 'I'm merely a local policeman doing his job.'

'You're too modest, Inspector,' said Danforth. 'I hear you've pulled off quite a few coups.'

De Silva was puzzled. How did the actor know anything about his career in Nuala?

Danforth laughed. 'I like to know what goes on in the places we visit, Inspector. Our new colleagues from your Amateur Dramatic Society have proved to be a mine of information about local affairs.'

Then Danforth was unusual, de Silva reflected. In his experience, most of the British who came to Ceylon were only interested in what went on in the country insofar as it impacted on their plans to govern or profit.

A twinkle came into Danforth's eyes, as if he read de Silva's mind. 'You may have realised from my accent that I'm not an Englishman, Inspector. My ways and opinions are not necessarily the same as theirs.'

Ah, that accounted for the accent. 'What is your nationality then, sir?' he asked.

'I'm Irish; but it's many years since I set foot in the Emerald Isle.'

An Irishman: that was interesting. In his schooldays, history lessons had focused on the achievements of the British Empire and England's glorious past. The brief mentions of British rule in Ireland had not portrayed the Irish in a favourable light. But looking at it from the standpoint of another occupied land, his own, he suspected that the Irish might feel much the same about the British as the British did about them. Still, politics was a subject best avoided with a man who was little more than a stranger to him. He cast around for something neutral to say.

'A charming name,' he came up with. 'Sometimes people call my country the Cinnamon Isle.'

Danforth smiled. 'Equally charming. From now on I shall imagine I smell the spice on the breeze. Our great Irish writer, James Joyce, likened Shakespeare's wife to sweet, fresh cinnamon until she grew old and ceased to be comely.' He clapped de Silva on the shoulder. 'But I don't expect you read *Ulysses*. Why should you? Tell me now, what did you think of our play?'

'I liked it very much. So much fine language and your sword fight at the end with Ophelia's brother, Laertes, was most dramatic.'

'Ah, the sword fight. Have you ever tried that kind of thing yourself, Inspector?'

'When I trained in Colombo, I had the chance to attempt it and found the experience most enlivening. Of course, we were mainly instructed in the use of firearms and defending ourselves against knife attacks.'

'Very good, sir. Mind you, it's just as well that the text allows for me not being as fit as I once was. Frank Sheridan, who plays Laertes, is very accomplished. He learnt to fence as a schoolboy and won several cups.' Danforth tucked Emerald Watson's arm into his. 'Unlike me, this is the first time Emerald has appeared in Hamlet. She did a tremendous job, don't you think?'

'I do.'

'She's only been with the company for a few months,' Danforth added.

'In fact,' Emerald chimed in, 'this is the first time I've ever been away from England. It's all so exciting.'

De Silva wondered how old she was. Not much more than twenty if he was any judge. 'I'm honoured that you chose to visit Ceylon for your first venture, Miss Watson.'

'Emerald, please.' She favoured him with a warm smile.

'My dear,' intervened Danforth. 'If we're to get to these caves that Mrs Clutterbuck recommends, we should be on our way. We have the dress rehearsal for our next offering this evening, Inspector. I decided it was best to allow my cast to rest in the heat of the day and work when it's cooler.'

'Very wise, sir. Nothing could be more pleasant than a drive out of town in your very fine car.'

'I'm glad you approve, although I have to admit, it doesn't belong to me. I hired it in Colombo for our stay. I thought it would be amusing to have a change of transport.' He smiled. 'And the ladies tell me they are enjoying the respite from our old bone-shaker of a bus.'

'If you intend to visit the Nuala Caves, it is a good choice for a hot afternoon. You'll find the temperature there more refreshing than in town and there's a magnificent statue of the Buddha in the main chamber.'

'So Mrs Clutterbuck tells me. We're looking forward to seeing it.'

He put out a hand to shake de Silva's once more. 'A pleasure to meet you, sir. I hope there will be other occasions.'

Watching the pair of them return to the car and drive away in a cloud of dust, de Silva pondered the little encounter. Alexander Danforth must have plenty of money to be able to hire a car like that. De Silva wondered if he had private means. Surely a travelling theatre company wasn't all that profitable.

He was undeniably a handsome man too, and Emerald Watson was very pretty. It was probably an innocent friendship but it was rather odd that he had chosen to do his sightseeing with her, rather than his wife. No explanation had been offered, and he gave every indication of being the kind of man who felt no need to justify his actions, but he might be putting Miss Watson in an awkward position. Jane would say one shouldn't spread gossip, and she'd be right, but there were plenty of people in Nuala, Florence Clutterbuck among them, who liked to indulge in it.

He returned to the Morris, and, with a few brisk words, scattered the crowd of small boys who had gathered round to inspect it while he had been otherwise occupied. They ran off whooping like a troupe of monkeys, and he grinned after them. He didn't blame them for admiring the car. Its smart navy paintwork and gleaming chrome were looking their best today, freshly washed and polished early that morning by two of his servants.

The drive to the police station was a slow crawl through the usual mêlée of lumbering bullock carts, darting rickshaws, and wayward pedestrians. The hill country had been having unusually hot weather for the past week: weather that was normally reserved for April. As de Silva waited for a cart laden with fruit and vegetables to move out of his way, he pulled a handkerchief from his pocket and mopped his brow.

The cart passed and he had just started to edge forward when he noticed a European woman he didn't recognise hovering at the far side of the road. She wore a dark costume with a high collar that emphasised the ramrod thinness of her figure. The shadow cast by her hat made it hard to see her face clearly, but the general impression he received was one of unbending severity and independence. Nevertheless, it was unusual to see a white woman alone in the bazaar. She might need help. He was just wondering whether he should stop and offer it when she turned briskly on her heel and disappeared into the throng.

At the station, Sergeant Prasanna and Constable Nadar stood to attention when he walked in, both of them swiftly doing up the top buttons of their uniform tunics. They looked as warm as he felt. He nodded as they chorused a good morning.

'Anything to report?'

Prasanna shook his head. 'No, sir. It has been quiet since we arrived.'

De Silva glanced at the pile of papers at Nadar's end of the counter. Something that looked suspiciously like a wooden elephant peeped over the top of them. He reached out and moved them aside to find there was also a small, sharp knife and a little pile of wood shavings and dust. He debated ticking Nadar off but it was too hot, so instead he picked the elephant up and studied it carefully, allowing his constable to stew a little before giving him a friendly smile. 'For your baby son, I suppose?'

A flicker of relief displaced the look of anxiety on Nadar's face. 'Yes, sir. I was only putting the finishing touches. It won't happen again.'

'I'm glad to hear it. Now get on and find yourselves something useful to do, starting with bringing me my tea. I have a throat full of dust after the drive here.'

'Right away, sir.'

In his office, he opened the letters on his desk and flipped through them. How much the British liked their paperwork. Orders, reports, regulations – always something to be reading and then filing, never to be seen again. He mourned the waste of trees.

Leaning back in his chair, he yawned. He had his regular monthly meeting with Archie Clutterbuck after lunch. He hoped the assistant government agent would be in a good mood. It would be nice to get the business over quickly and go home.

* * *

The recently ended monsoon rains had given new luxuriance to the Residence's gardens and, as the Morris proceeded up the drive, de Silva admired the greenness of the lawns and the profusion of the flower borders. A servant showed him straight to the study where Clutterbuck stood behind his desk, caught in the act of loosening his tie. De Silva couldn't help noticing that the latter was a strong shade of yellow, very different from Clutterbuck's usual choices of burgundy, brown or muted green. His manner was also more than usually affable, especially in view of the heat. De Silva was well aware that it normally made him somewhat cantankerous. He must have had good news, or perhaps a win on the horses. It was rare for there to be nothing that he wanted to haul one up on, however mildly.

'Damned hot,' Clutterbuck observed, unnecessarily. He gestured to the elderly Labrador flopped on the polished floor near an open window. 'Poor old Darcy feels it too. Now, anything in particular you'd like to discuss?'

'Only small matters, sir. In general, everything in town has been quiet.'

'Excellent. Let's make ourselves comfortable first.'

He walked over to the bay window and sat down in one of the leather armchairs, indicating that de Silva should take the other one. Picking up the dish on the low table in between, he held it out. 'You must try some of these cheese straws. Mrs Clutterbuck's cook makes very tasty ones and sometimes I like a snack while I'm at work.'

If Clutterbuck's ever-expanding girth was anything to go by, de Silva suspected that he liked a snack most of the time.

Ensconced in his chair, de Silva accepted a cheese straw and took a bite. 'You're right, sir,' he said when he had eaten it and wiped his lips. 'Very tasty, but also crumbly.'

'Ah, never mind a few crumbs, de Silva. Darcy will clear those up before long. So, fire away then.'

De Silva went through the police matters that had come up since their last discussion, then, business over, listened patiently while Clutterbuck regaled him with tales of his latest fishing trip to Horton Plains. Fishing was a pursuit that troubled de Silva's Buddhist principles less than some of the other recreations in which Clutterbuck liked to indulge. After all, fishermen usually ate what they caught and the Buddha had not entirely prohibited the eating of flesh. It was harder to forgive the taking of the life of an elephant or a leopard. He had never heard of either of their sad carcasses being destined for the table.

Idly, he admired how the rays of sunshine passing through the stained-glass crests that decorated the bay window cast patches of red, blue, and yellow onto the table and the floor. Darcy grunted and stretched then lumbered to his feet, only to waddle to a cooler area of the room and flop down again. He looked as lethargic as de Silva felt, what with the heat and the drone of Clutterbuck's voice.

With a superhuman effort, he pulled his attention back to the monologue. Now Clutterbuck was airing his opinions on the fishing flies one should use. Even though de Silva was not interested in fishing, he found the names had a charm of their own. Royal Coachman, Parmachene Belle, Ginger Quill. It was hard to imagine Clutterbuck's large, meaty hands engaged in the delicate art of tying the requisite scraps of feather and fur to the menacing little hooks that would snare his quarry.

There was a knock and a servant entered. Clutterbuck looked up. 'Yes?'

'The memsahib has sent me to say tea is served, sahib.'

Clutterbuck hoisted himself out of his chair. De Silva felt some sympathy for his resigned expression.

'If there's nothing more that we need to discuss, de Silva…'

'I don't think so, sir.'

De Silva rose too, glad he would soon be back at Sunnybank and able to change out of his uniform. Today, it felt as if every piece of it clung to him with unwelcome friendliness.

'Good, then we'll wrap this up.' Clutterbuck nodded to the servant. 'Tell the memsahib I'll be with her in a minute.'

Gratefully, de Silva said farewell. He was looking forward

to spending what was left of the afternoon at Sunnybank.

As he emerged onto the sunlit drive, he noticed one of the Clutterbucks' servants walking Florence's dog, Angel. The man looked apprehensive, as well he might. Angel was a feisty little creature with a reputation for nipping ankles, although, on their occasional meetings, he had given de Silva no trouble.

His path to the Morris crossed with that of Angel and his minder. The little dog wagged its tail uncertainly and then held up a paw. The servant gave de Silva a lopsided grin.

'Would you like to take charge of him, sahib? I believe he is happy to see you.'

'I can't imagine why he should be.' Then he remembered the cheese straws. Perhaps a few crumbs still lingered on his trousers. He brushed his hands down his legs and the little dog strained forward, its black, button nose snuffling about on the ground. When it finished, it gazed up at de Silva, tail wagging once more. De Silva bent down to pat its fluffy head. 'I haven't anything else,' he said with a smile. 'But I'm sure you're well fed here.'

The servant rolled his eyes. 'Like a prince, sahib. The memsahib says everything must be the best.'

'I'm sure she does. Well, enjoy your walk.'

'Thank you, sahib. I will try.'

De Silva watched for a moment as they walked away, Angel darting about on the lead in a manner that would surely not have been approved of at the famous Crufts dog show. But then it was generally known that the little creature was like a child to Florence Clutterbuck, and one that was never told off.

At home, Jane was already ensconced on the verandah, a book open in her lap. She smiled up at him, shading her eyes against the sun. 'Hello, dear, you're early. Do I gather that it went well at the Residence?'

He bent down and kissed her cheek. 'Yes, very well. Archie was in an unusually cheery mood.'

'That's good.'

He yawned. 'But he kept me sitting there while he talked about fishing when I would rather have been home with you.'

'Well, you're here now. Shall we have some tea?'

'Excellent idea. And a slice of butter cake would go down nicely too.'

'There should be a fresh one. Cook was baking this morning.'

She rang the bell on the small table at her side and a servant appeared. De Silva settled down in pleasant antici-pation of his favourite sweet treat.

'I've had a very quiet afternoon,' Jane remarked. 'I'd planned to get on with that altar cloth I'm stitching for the church, but just the thought of all those folds of material in my lap made me feel too hot. I shall have to tell Florence it won't be finished for another week. Did you see her at the Residence this afternoon?'

'There was no sign of her, but she must have been about. I escaped from my meeting with Archie thanks to a servant reminding him he was expected at the tea table. I did see one of the servants walking her dog though.'

Jane raised an eyebrow. 'She must be suffering from the heat; she and Angel are usually inseparable. She even brings him to the sewing circle. I could see that poor Mrs Carterton who was hosting us last week didn't like it at all. Angel barked so much at her cat that it fled into the garden and didn't come back for two days.'

He told her about his encounter with Angel.

'You've obviously made a new friend,' she said when he came to the end of the story. 'Most dogs adore cheese. Anything else to report?'

'I came across the famous Alexander Danforth in town. He nearly ran me down in his expensive Lagonda.'

'Goodness, are you alright?'

'Oh yes, he missed. He did stop and apologised profusely.'

'I should jolly well hope so.'

'But it would have been even better if he'd offered me a spin in his car.'

'I do believe you're a little envious, Shanti.'

'Well... No, I wouldn't part with the Morris for anything.'

'Was Mrs Danforth with him?'

No, he was with Miss Watson, the young lady who played Ophelia. They were off to the caves to do some sightseeing.'

'How nice. I expect his wife isn't interested in caves and statues. Or with that lovely creamy skin of hers, she probably prefers to keep out of the sun. Redheads have to be so careful of burning and I don't expect she wants to spoil her complexion with freckles.'

'The niceties of the female complexion and the magic potions used to preserve it are a closed book to me,' he said with a smile.

She shot him a glance of mock reproof over the rim of her reading glasses. 'You're very provoking.'

He grinned. 'It's part of my charm.'

'Did you find out anything else?'

'About what?'

'The Danforths, of course.'

'Umm... Let me see... Ah yes, he told me he's Irish, although he hasn't lived there for a long time. I didn't ask if his wife is as well.'

'He didn't sound Irish when he played Hamlet. He must have lost the accent.'

'I don't think so. I noticed a difference straight away when we met. But I expect that is what acting is about.'

Jane sniffed.

'It was very pleasant to listen to,' de Silva said. 'Gentle like an old song.'

'Then he must be from the south. The accent in the north is quite a harsh one. Well, perhaps we'll come across him again before they leave Nuala. I must say, I'd love to hear about his adventures.'

* * *

After dinner, they sat in the drawing room and read in companionable silence. Inspired by the performance of Hamlet, de Silva had decided to try more of Shakespeare's work and, at Jane's suggestion, had chosen to read some of the sonnets. He started with the one that Jane said she liked the best. It began *Let me not to the marriage of true minds admit impediment…*

He paused on that final word, liking its feeling of weight and the way it enhanced the meaning. It appeared also in the words the vicar had used when he and Jane married four years ago. *If any man knows any just cause or impediment why these two people should not be joined together, let him speak now or forever hold his peace.*

For a moment, his nerves had jangled. Because the vicar at the church Jane attended was a man of liberal views, out of kindness, he had agreed to perform a service very close to the traditional one. But what if a voice boomed down the aisle of that cool, quiet church, forbidding the union of an Anglican Englishwoman and a Sinhalese Buddhist? Fortunately, the service passed uninterrupted and they and the small congregation drawn from the family where Jane had been employed as a governess, and the colleagues in the Colombo force he counted as friends, had departed happily for a celebration at a nearby hotel.

He read on but his eyelids began to droop. 'I think I'll take my usual turn round the garden before bed,' he remarked.

Jane looked up from her book. 'I just have one more chapter. I know I won't sleep until I find out who did it.'

'Then I'll leave you to finish.'

He was at the top of the stairs leading to the garden when he heard the telephone ring in the house. He frowned. At this time of the evening?

'Oh dear, I hope it's nothing serious,' said Jane. A servant came to the door. 'It is Sahib Clutterbuck, sahib. He says it is urgent.'

The authoritative tone had returned to Clutterbuck's voice. 'De Silva? You'd better get over to the theatre straight away.'

De Silva frowned. 'Now, sir?'

'Yes, now. It can't wait until morning. I wasn't here when they called or I would have rung you sooner. Alexander Danforth was found dead in his dressing room a few hours ago.'

The furrow between de Silva's eyebrows deepened. The man had looked as fit as a fiddle that afternoon.

'Dead? Was there an accident?'

'An accident? No, we have a murder on our hands. Now, hurry up, de Silva. I'll meet you there.'

Strange, thought de Silva, as he replaced the receiver. Why was it that the Residence had been informed before the police?

CHAPTER 3

De Silva parked the Morris in the dusty, treeless parking area behind the theatre and walked over to join Clutter-buck who waited for him at the stage door.

'I'm afraid this is bound to get out sooner or later,' Clutterbuck said over his shoulder as he led the way inside. 'But I'd prefer it to be later. At the moment, apart from Doctor Hebden and ourselves, only the members of the company and the caretaker on duty are in the know.' He indicated a booth to their left. 'That's his place if we need him.'

'Who found the body?'

'Not Mrs Danforth, thank goodness. It was one of the men – that fellow Sheridan.'

De Silva remembered the name. Frank Sheridan was the actor who played the ghost of Hamlet's father, and Ophelia's avenging brother, Laertes.

Unlike the public areas, the corridor they walked down was shabby and the rooms he glanced into as he passed looked no better, although the smell of sawdust and new paint assailed his nostrils. Presumably, it came from recent construction and painting of the scenery for Danforth's performances. He wouldn't have any need of that now. Briefly, de Silva wondered what the company would do without its leader.

They reached the far end of the corridor and Clutterbuck

pushed open a door with his foot. He stood aside to let de Silva enter. The sight that met his eyes reminded him of many of the scenes that he had witnessed in his years in the Colombo force. Violent death had been a frequent occurrence there; something he hoped he had left behind when he and Jane moved to Nuala.

Danforth's body was slumped over his dressing table. His legs were bare but a loose black robe, patterned with gold dragons, covered his upper half. His head was face down in a soup of creams, liquids and powders that had spilt from the pots and jars scattered randomly over the dressing table's surface. But the main ingredient in the soup was blood, and it was easy to see where it stemmed from. The blades of a large pair of scissors had been driven deep into the man's neck, just below the curve of the jawbone. De Silva estimated that the person who had wielded those scissors had found his victim's carotid artery with lethal exactitude. Blood was also on the mirror where someone had daubed four words in large letters. The flow of the blood had distorted them but they could still be read:

the rest is silence

'Has anything been touched?' he asked.

'I gave strict instructions when I arrived that nothing was to be interfered with, but I can't vouch for what happened before then. Do you think there's a chance of getting any fingerprints off those scissors?'

De Silva looked at them doubtfully. 'It may be possible, but I won't be able to lift a complete print from the curved surface of the handles and it wouldn't surprise me if they've already been wiped, or the murderer wore gloves.'

Clutterbuck nodded sagely. 'Do your best.' He rubbed

his chin. 'No evidence of a struggle. It looks as if he went down like a felled tree. Do you think he was knocked out first?'

De Silva bent over the tangled mass of dark hair. His hands became sticky with blood as he carefully parted it in a few places. He noticed a faint aroma of brandy.

'No,' he said after a few moments, going to wash his hands in the basin in one corner of the room. 'There's no sign of a blow. But I agree it's very unlikely his assailant would have been able to stab him without a struggle. The most likely explanation is that he was drugged in some way.'

'Hebden should be able to help us with that. I telephoned him after I spoke to you. He's on his way.' He cocked an ear as they heard the approach of brisk footsteps along the corridor. 'Ah, that might be him now.'

The door opened and Doctor Hebden came in. A tall man, and usually irreproachable in his dress, tonight his suit appeared to have been donned in a considerable hurry and his hair looked hastily combed. Perhaps, like de Silva, he had planned an early night. He stopped in the doorway for a moment, taking in the scene, then put his battered black bag on a nearby chair. 'Good evening, sir.' He nodded to de Silva. 'Inspector.'

Clutterbuck stepped forward. 'As you see, Hebden, we have a problem on our hands.'

Hebden approached Danforth's body, put a capable-looking hand on the dead man's ashen cheek and then lifted one of the eyelids. 'No onset of rigor mortis yet,' he remarked. 'When was he found?'

'At about six o'clock this evening. The professional actors were due to have the dress rehearsal for their next production. The Residence wasn't alerted for an hour or so – I imagine there was a bit of a fuss.'

De Silva raised a mental eyebrow at the typical British

understatement, as if the butler had served burnt toast at breakfast.

'As bad luck would have it,' Clutterbuck continued, 'my wife and I were out at a dinner, hence the delay in notifying you and de Silva. It won't cause a problem, will it?'

De Silva wondered whether to ask who had raised the alarm but decided to leave that for now.

'Not at all, sir,' said Hebden. 'It just means I won't be able to make arrangements for the body to be removed and an autopsy arranged until the morning, but I can make a preliminary examination now.'

'Good man. How can we help?'

Hebden studied Danforth's body carefully. 'I'd like to get the scissors out and move him to that bed over there.' He indicated a low divan in a corner of the dressing room. 'Do you have any objection, Inspector? If you're hoping to find fingerprints, I have gloves.'

De Silva nodded. 'Thank you. If you'll excuse me a few moments, I'll go out to my car and fetch the fingerprinting equipment and a bag.'

Outside, the stars burned with fierce brightness in the night sky; the moon sailed between rags of cloud. De Silva rummaged in the glove compartment for the torch he kept there, switched it on, and found the box where he kept a small selection of items that might come in useful at the scene of a crime. From it, he extracted his fingerprinting equipment, gloves, and an evidence bag.

When he had replaced the box, he locked the car and paused for a few moments. In truth, he was glad to get some fresh air. No matter how many times he witnessed the aftermath of violent death, the ugliness of it still affected him. He thought of that fine-looking, energetic man he had met in the bazaar, so full of vitality and bonhomie. It was chilling to think that his life had been brutally snuffed out. He inhaled sharply then started to walk back to the theatre.

In Danforth's dressing room, Hebden was still in the process of removing the scissors; the blades had penetrated deeply. 'Whoever did this must have exerted considerable force,' he remarked.

'A man, do you think?' asked Clutterbuck.

Hebden shrugged. 'It could be a woman with strength and determination. I wouldn't rule it out.'

'De Silva thinks Danforth may have been drugged before the attack.'

'The autopsy should confirm whether that's the case.' He gave the scissors a final tug and held them up in his gloved hand. More blood seeped from the wound. 'Here you are, Inspector.'

De Silva took the scissors carefully and wiped away the blood, then laid them on a piece of cloth. He took a round, squirrel hairbrush from his kit and dipped it into a box of powder, then rotated it slowly over the uppermost side of the scissors, sifting the powder onto the metal. Finally, he unrolled a length of tape and pressed it neatly over the powdered surface before lifting it off gently. He inspected the underside of the tape. As he had expected: nothing. He repeated the process on the other side of the scissors but to no avail.

He shrugged. 'It was worth a try, but I'm afraid there's nothing to help us here.' He dusted off the scissors and dropped them into the evidence bag.

'Well,' said Hebden. 'If you're ready, gentlemen?'

It was an awkward job to pull out the chair with Danforth's weight on it and then carry him to the divan, but, eventually, it was done. Clutterbuck wiped his glistening forehead with his handkerchief and de Silva felt his own heart beat a little faster than usual. He knew that David Hebden was a keen sportsman. Perhaps that was why his part in the manoeuvre appeared to have left him unruffled. Maybe Jane was right about taking more exercise.

He watched as Hebden went over the body, sponging away blood where necessary, to give it his preliminary examination. 'I agree with your conclusion,' he said after a few minutes. 'When Danforth was attacked, he must have already been in no condition to put up a fight. Apart from the obvious wound to the neck, his body's unblemished.'

He snapped off his bloodstained gloves. 'The best I can do tonight is cover him with a sheet. I'll get the hospital to send an ambulance in the morning and transfer him to the mortuary.'

Clutterbuck glanced at the door and nodded. 'There's a key, so the room can be locked.'

A sheet lay folded at the foot of the bed. Hebden shook it out and draped it over Danforth's body then straightened up. 'Well, I'll be on my way.'

'Thank you for coming out. Let's speak again tomorrow,' said Clutterbuck.

He turned to de Silva as the door closed behind the doctor. 'Naturally, Mrs Danforth was terribly shocked, so I've already sent her back to her hotel with her maid. Miss Watson has gone too. If you have questions for any of them, they'll have to wait. Where ladies are concerned, I'm sure you'll agree that every consideration must be given. Fortunately, none of the members of the amateur dramatic group were in the building but the male members of the company are still here. I suggest you see them briefly then let them return to their hotel. You can interview them fully in the morning. A few hours won't make any difference.'

Gallantry was all very well, but de Silva felt a twinge of annoyance that Clutterbuck had so rapidly taken matters into his own hands. Doubtless the ladies were very distressed but, after a crime, it was always useful to observe the behaviour of anyone who might be a suspect before they had time to compose themselves. Perhaps Clutterbuck wanted to get home to bed himself and that had clouded his judgement, but there was no point in making an issue of it now.

'Very well, sir, but I think I'll stay and look around for a while afterwards.'

Clutterbuck shrugged. 'As you wish. The men are assembled in the green room. Do you know where that is?'

De Silva shook his head. He wasn't even familiar with the term, but he wished Clutterbuck had observed the elementary precaution of keeping the men apart. At this stage, they were all suspects. His superior's judgement really was questionable tonight. He wondered how many times the port had passed after the ladies withdrew from the dining room at the dinner he had attended.

The room that Clutterbuck led him to was painted a grimy beige rather than green. The term must be another of those strange British expressions, reflected de Silva. As they entered, five men of varying ages stopped their conversation and looked up. The scene had an incongruous air for they were all dressed in eighteenth-century costume, presumably on account of the planned rehearsal. Clutterbuck's brusque introductions gave the impression that he didn't consider any of them to be his equal, but de Silva resolved to treat them with respect.

'As you are aware, gentlemen,' he began, 'Alexander Danforth was found murdered in his dressing room earlier this evening.' He nodded to the man who had been introduced as Frank Sheridan. 'I understand that it was you who found the body.'

There was a wintry expression on Sheridan's narrow face, its anguish accentuated by a high-bridged nose and thin lips. 'Yes,' he said grimly. He jabbed a hand through the dark hair that was plastered to his head. Presumably, he had only recently discarded one of the powdered wigs that de Silva saw lying on a low table nearby.

'It must have been a terrible shock.'

'It was. We were due to begin our final rehearsal, and everyone was assembled here. It was unlike Alexander to be late. He was always the consummate professional.'

'So you went to his dressing room to see what was wrong.'

'Yes. I found him dead and came straight back here to get help.'

'And then what happened?'

'There was confusion for a while. None of us were sure what to do. Morville told the caretaker to contact the police station but there was no reply. Unsurprising, I suppose, as it was nearly eight o'clock. It was Mrs Danforth who said we should telephone the Residence, but I was told the Clutterbucks were out.'

That was one little mystery cleared up, thought de Silva. 'And how did you fill the time until Mr Clutterbuck arrived here?'

'Mrs Danforth and Miss Watson went to lie down. The rest of us just stayed here. We didn't talk much. I think we were all in shock.'

'Are you saying that no one went back into the dressing room and disturbed anything?'

'Not quite. Raikes came back in with me but we were careful to leave everything as we found it.'

'Thank you, sir. And is that how the rest of you gentlemen remember it?'

Paul Mayne, the actor who had played Hamlet's friend, Horatio, snorted impatiently. 'It was only a few hours ago, Inspector. I think you can safely assume that.'

De Silva regarded him coolly. 'In my line of work, sir, I find it advisable never to assume anything.'

Mayne had the grace to mumble an apology.

'All our nerves are on edge, Inspector,' Michael Morville interposed. De Silva recalled that he had played Polonius, Ophelia's bumbling father, who came to a sticky end behind a tapestry after being mistaken by Hamlet for the villain, King Claudius. 'Sheridan's account matches what I remember. It was just before six when he went to the dressing room to call Alexander. He was gone less than a minute when we heard him shout, then he rushed in and told us the terrible news.'

'You were quite certain Mr Danforth was already dead?'

'Dead as a doornail,' one of the other men said. 'I saw enough of it in the war to be sure of that.'

'Thank you, Mr Raikes,' Clutterbuck said dryly. 'You will have realised Mr Raikes was not one of the actors, de Silva,' he added.

'Stage manager, and jack of all bloody trades, that's me,' said Raikes gruffly.

'Thank you, sir. Can you tell me who the last person to see Mr Danforth alive was?'

'Me and Sheridan.'

'And what time would that have been?'

The two men looked at each other. 'Around four o'clock, Bert?'

'Sounds about right.'

'I was discussing some theatre business with Alexander,' Sheridan went on. 'Bert came in to replace a couple of light bulbs on the dressing table mirror. Alexander was always meticulous about doing his stage makeup in a good light. After that, we left him to rest or go over his lines before he started to get ready for the rehearsal. No one, not even Kathleen, disturbed Alexander when he was resting. Company rule – we all knew that.'

'Where did you go then?'

'Back to my dressing room.'

'And I had some props to see to down that side,' Bert Raikes chimed in.

De Silva turned to the fifth man, Charles Crichton. He remembered he had acted the part of King Claudius in the play. He was an imposing fellow with a deep, resonant voice. 'What about you, sir? Do you have anything more to tell us?'

Crichton raised his eyes to the ceiling. 'A tragedy, my dear Inspector. A great soul has departed this mortal coil. A man I was proud to call a friend—'

'Thank you, Crichton,' Clutterbuck intervened testily. 'But I think we've all had enough for one night. It's nearly one o'clock.'

Crichton looked nettled.

'I suggest you go back to your hotel, gentlemen,' Clutterbuck continued. 'The inspector and I would be obliged if you would stay there until further notice. I'm sure he'll have more questions for you in due course.'

The men trooped out. When the door closed behind them, Clutterbuck gave a snort. 'What a buffoon. That type can never remember they're not on stage. As for the rest, Sheridan and Raikes seem decent enough chaps, and Morville appears to be harmless, but you'll have to curb that puppy Mayne.'

De Silva held his peace. True to his word, he preferred not to make assumptions.

'Well, it's a start,' Clutterbuck went on. He smothered a yawn. 'We'll talk tomorrow, or rather later today. You should get off home now. I intend to.'

'Thank you, sir, but if you have no objection, I'd still like to have a look round and speak to the caretaker before I go.'

'As you wish.' Clutterbuck headed for the door. 'Goodnight, de Silva.'

'Goodnight, sir.'

Left alone, he went to find the caretaker. The man was sitting in his booth, calmly filling in a puzzle in a copy of the *Nuala Times* that looked several days old. His jaws worked steadily and de Silva smelt the oily odour of a betel quid, the little parcel of areca nuts, lime and spices wrapped in betel leaf that so many locals were fond of chewing for the lift it gave to their mood. He supposed there was no reason why the man shouldn't take the night's events in his stride. After all, what was a dead Britisher to him?

'The front doors to the theatre have been locked since the last performance,' he said in reply to de Silva's question.

'That would be the performance of Hamlet on Saturday night?'

'Yes, sahib.'

'Would anyone who wanted to get into the theatre have to come in by the stage door then?'

'There is a side entrance to the foyer for deliveries to the bar.'

'Could someone get from there to the auditorium?'

The caretaker shook his head. 'When there is no performance, the doors between them are locked as the owner wishes, and I have the keys.'

'Do you see everyone who comes in by the stage door?'

'Yes.'

'But there must be times when you are not here.'

'If I am elsewhere in the theatre, I lock up. Otherwise, if I cannot be here because I am sick, the old man will come and take my place.'

'The old man?'

'Prathiv. Before I came, he worked here as the caretaker for many years.'

De Silva glanced around the lobby; two corridors led off it in opposing directions. He already knew that the one to the left when one entered by the stage door led to the Danforths' dressing rooms and the green room. He asked about the one to the right.

'It is the way to the rest of the dressing rooms, sahib. They are smaller than the ones belonging to Sahib and Memsahib Danforth.'

'Was everyone except for them at the right-hand end of

the theatre that afternoon, particularly after four o'clock?'

The caretaker shrugged. 'The one with the thin face who does not speak passed by, going to the left side, but I think he returned by four.'

That sounded like Sheridan, thought de Silva. 'Sahib Raikes went out for a time,' the man went on. 'He stopped to speak with me and said he was going to buy something in the bazaar.'

'What was that?'

'He asked where he might find nails and paint, sahib.'

'Did you see him come back?'

'Of course. He said he had to change a light bulb in Sahib Danforth's dressing room, but he was not gone for long. Then he went back to the right. There is a room down there he uses as a workshop. After that it was quiet until it was time for everyone to move to the green room.'

'Did Mr Raikes go to the green room too? Even though he's not one of the actors?'

'Yes. He stands in the wings, sahib, in case he is needed, and to remind the actors if they forget their lines.'

'Is there any way someone could cross from one corridor to the other without passing here?'

'I do not think so, sahib, but Prathiv would know for certain. As I told you, he has been here many years.'

De Silva thanked him and returned to Danforth's dressing room. There weren't many drawers to look through and only one cupboard, which was empty apart from the costumes Danforth had worn in Hamlet and a few shirts and trousers, but a large trunk and numerous suitcases and boxes were distributed around the room. He looked at them despondently, with dawning awareness of the size of the task he had undertaken at such a late hour. Well, he might as well get on with it.

Snapping open the metal catches on one of the smaller suitcases, he inspected the contents: scripts, posters, and playbills for future shows. Another case contained all kinds of footwear, from leather boots that made de Silva think of *The Three Musketeers* to two-tone Oxfords and smart brogues.

Numerous suitcases, and nearly an hour later, he stopped to roll his stiff shoulders. Not many more to go now; the end was in sight. In the last but one case, a holdall really, he found a folder containing a thick wad of letters. Mainly, they concerned the company's bookings and there was nothing interesting about them. Some were several years old and their relevance doubtful. He wondered why Danforth had kept them, but then he noticed that they all covered only one side of the paper they were written on. Danforth had used the blank, reverse sides for notes and lists.

De Silva glanced at the silent, sheeted figure on the bed in the corner. It was strangely touching that this flamboyant man had possessed such a thrifty trait. A small thing that revealed an unexpected element to his character. His writing was neat too, taking up an economical amount of space. De Silva supposed he shouldn't be surprised. It must have taken considerable powers of organisation to transport the theatre company halfway round the world. The combination of those organisational skills with an outgoing, warm personality and artistic flair was interesting. De Silva felt sorry that he hadn't had the chance to know the man better.

Next, he tackled the dressing rooms used by the other male actors and Miss Watson. Fortunately, they didn't take him so long, even though he was scrupulously thorough. He moved on to adjacent storerooms that held decades of costumes and accoutrements from the theatre's heyday. Delving into cupboards and chests, he found breastplates and helmets sharing space with crinolines and fans; Roman togas with flapper dresses; doublets and hose with tennis whites, and elaborate Elizabethan, Georgian and Regency gowns with saucy sailor suits. As he worked, he disturbed

37

ghostly armies of moths and flourishing societies of dust mites.

He had left Kathleen Danforth's dressing room until last and found that there was also a small room beyond it that appeared to be a workroom for her maid. A daunting array of clothes, shoes, accessories, wigs, beauty preparations, and makeup met his eyes. Astringent scents mingled with musky and flowery ones. The musky aroma was particularly strong in the workroom. He wondered if Kathleen Danforth's maid was fond of "borrowing" some of her mistress's expensive perfume.

Used to Jane's practical approach to matters of feminine embellishments, he embarked on his task with trepidation. Nevertheless, in the pursuit of thoroughness, when he had finished with the rest of the room, he even cast a glance into the wastepaper basket, but there was nothing in it but wads of used cotton wool and a few withered stems of yellow roses with a small card on top of them. It was signed "Bunnikins" followed by two kisses. It might be a pet name she and Danforth used.

He stretched: he'd done enough for tonight. It was time he went home and got some sleep. It wasn't until he emerged into the parking area that he realised that the company's bus had gone without a search. The men must have taken it back to their hotel. It wasn't ideal, but he was too tired to follow now. It would have to wait.

* * *

Dawn was coming up by the time he reached Sunnybank. His beloved garden shimmered in the early morning light and crimson streaked the sky.

Jane must have been listening for the car, for she greeted him in the hall in her dressing gown.

'Shanti! What a night of it you've had.'

He sighed. 'It has been rather a long one.'

'Shall I get the servants to fetch coffee and something to eat?'

'Yes please, anything will do.'

As he ate, he recounted the night's events. 'Horrible,' she said with a shudder when he told her of how Danforth had died. 'I must say, I agree with you that he was probably drugged first. A strong man like him would surely have put up a fight – unless someone was very clever and surprised him completely.'

'Like a cat burglar?'

'Yes.'

'Whoever it was, I think he must have been a pretty chilly customer to risk killing Danforth when any of the company might have come in and disturbed him, in spite of the company rule I was told of.'

'A cool customer, dear,' Jane said mildly. 'And are you sure it was a *him*? There are two women in the company, don't forget.'

'Three, if you count Mrs Danforth's maid. But one of those women, Miss Watson, was at the other end of the theatre, so if the men couldn't pass the caretaker without being seen, neither could she. As for Mrs Danforth—'

'It's hard to imagine anyone so beautiful committing such an ugly crime, but don't forget Lady Macbeth. Often the wife is the villain. I've read dozens of novels where that's been the case.'

De Silva shrugged. 'It's true that the murderer is frequently someone close to the victim.'

She poured him some more coffee. 'Scissors are more likely to be a woman's weapon than a man's, too.'

'And what is your evidence for that?'

'Intuition.'

'Another woman's weapon? It would need more than that to convince a judge and jury.'

She gave him an apologetic smile. 'I'm sorry, dear. I know I'm not taking this seriously enough. It's just it seems unreal somehow. These actors come to Nuala and perform a play about murder and revenge and then we have a real-life murder.' She rested her chin on her hand. 'Those words on the mirror—'

'The rest is silence?'

'Yes. Hamlet's last words after he kills Claudius. There must be a clue there and, although I can't really explain why, I don't think it's something a man would write. Did you ask anyone about them?'

'No time. Archie Clutterbuck was too keen to wrap things up. As I said, he'd already had Kathleen Danforth, her maid, and Miss Watson driven back to their hotel and he sent the men off too before I had time to question them in anything more than the most cursory fashion.'

'That strikes me as strange. After all, a murder in Nuala isn't exactly an everyday event. Perhaps he was tired out, but you always tell me you don't like to delay your questions and he ought to have respected that.'

'It's something I was taught very early in my career. People forget things if there's a delay. Little details that may be important. And the murderer has less time to compose himself, or herself. Sometimes immediate questioning draws out a clue as to the person who's guilty. If it had been up to me, I wouldn't have let the ladies leave before I had spoken to them, or permitted the men to be together before they were questioned.'

He brushed a few crumbs from his tunic and stood up. 'I need some sleep before I carry on trying to make sense of this.' He kissed the top of her head. 'I'll leave you and your ingenious mind to puzzle over the problem.'

'You're teasing me.'

'Not at all, you know I regard you as Nuala's answer to Miss Marple. I expect you to have the solution by lunchtime.'

CHAPTER 4

'I've made arrangements for the men to come up here so you can interview them in private,' said Clutterbuck.

They were in the study at the Residence. Outside, sunshine bathed the garden in golden light but, thankfully, today the room was cooler than on de Silva's last visit.

'It'll only cause a lot of speculation if they're seen coming to the police station,' Clutterbuck went on. 'And their hotel will probably be no better.'

De Silva was surprised but, provided he was allowed to conduct his investigations as he wanted, he saw no reason to object. 'What about the ladies?' he asked.

'That can wait.'

'I'd prefer it if there wasn't too much of a delay before I speak to them.'

'I appreciate that.' Clutterbuck's tone was irritable. 'Everything will be done properly, I assure you.'

De Silva didn't feel particularly reassured but he nodded his thanks. 'Very well then. If the gentlemen are already here, I'll make a start.'

'I suggest we begin with Sheridan, although he may not have much more to tell us.'

Clutterbuck led the way down a corridor that took them to a pokey room that was new to de Silva. There was no furniture apart from a table and three straight-backed chairs, two of them ranged on one side of the table and the third opposite. A notepad and a blue china pot containing a few pens and pencils stood on the table top, alongside a small brass hand bell. Clutterbuck picked up the bell and rang it. A moment later, a servant appeared in the doorway. 'You are ready to begin, sahib?' the man enquired.

'Yes. Ask Mr Sheridan to come in.'

He selected a pen and laid it across the notepad. 'You can do the talking, de Silva. For now, I simply want to observe. I'd like to get the measure of these fellows. I thought it might help to have the benefit of another pair of eyes. Gauge how they conduct themselves, and so forth. You can tell a lot about a man by watching him closely. Sometimes that's more revealing than what's actually said.'

'Indeed it is, sir.'

Clutterbuck sat down on one of the chairs facing away from the window. He gestured to de Silva to take the other.

'Make sure the light falls on their faces and not ours,' he remarked. 'Old trick. Puts a man at a disadvantage if he can't see his interlocutor too clearly.'

De Silva felt a twinge of discomfort. Whatever Clutterbuck said about leaving the questioning to him, it was clear he had no real intention of taking a back seat.

There was a knock at the door and the servant returned. 'Mr Sheridan is here, sahib.'

Frank Sheridan came into the room. He looked more composed than he had the previous evening and all traces of stage makeup had been wiped from his face. The eighteenth-century costume was replaced by khaki trousers and a soft-necked white shirt.

'Take a seat, Mr Sheridan,' said Clutterbuck, indicating the vacant chair. 'The inspector here has a few questions for you. Any light you can throw on this damnable business would be appreciated.'

Sheridan glanced at him sharply as he sat down. 'Light?

How much of that do you need to work out who stood to gain from Alexander's death?'

'Inspector de Silva will ask the questions.' Clutterbuck gave Sheridan a chilly stare. 'I strongly advise you against jumping to any conclusions.'

A flush darkened the actor's cheeks but he didn't make a riposte.

'Carry on, Inspector,' Clutterbuck said gruffly.

His attitude grated on de Silva and it also puzzled him. It certainly contrasted unfavourably with his attitude to the ladies in the company. Sheridan was hardly likely to open up when confronted with hostility. He took a breath. 'Mr Sheridan, I'd be grateful if you would go through yesterday's events for me once more, starting with your last conversation with Alexander Danforth.'

Sheridan looked as if he was tempted to reply with a dismissive remark but then thought better of it. 'I was with Alexander in his dressing room from about three o'clock. I'm not sure exactly how long I spent with him but it was probably around an hour.'

'Did he seem in good spirits?'

'Of course. Alexander was the kind of man who was rarely anything else. He took difficulties in his stride.'

'And were there any problems you needed to discuss?'

'Nothing of importance. Bookings were good for the rest of our stay in Nuala and most of the arrangements were made for our next port of call. There were a few minor problems with scenery and a trunk with some of our costumes went missing on the journey from Colombo. I suggested I go to the railway station to see if it had turned up, but Alexander wasn't worried. He knew Olive could always be relied on to find a way of plugging the gaps if necessary. She's very skilled with her needle.'

'Olive?'

'Olive Reilly, Mrs Danforth's maid.'

'And was Bert Raikes with you?'

'He came in to fix the lights. As I told you last night, Alexander was very particular about having a good light to do his stage makeup by.'

'Would you say that when you left Mr Danforth, there was nothing out of the ordinary going on?'

'Nothing at all, Inspector, and I fail to see where this is leading.'

'Just making sure I have the facts straight, sir.'

'Very well,' said Sheridan with a shrug.

'And after you and Mr Raikes left the dressing room, where did you go?'

'Straight to my dressing room. I wanted to run over my lines and compose myself before the rehearsal.'

'Did you stay there until it was time to go to the green room?'

'Yes.'

All of that tallied with what had been said the previous night. De Silva tried a different tack. 'How long have you known Mr Danforth?'

'Twenty years. We were in the same regiment during the war; we fought together in France.'

'Would you describe your relationship as a close one?'

'In war, Inspector, you soon get to know your companions. Those you take to quickly become fast friends. Alexander Danforth was one of those.'

'Then you knew him well?'

'Haven't I said so? In fact, if it wasn't for him, I wouldn't be here today. I owe him my life.'

De Silva let the hostile tone pass. He saw how Sheridan's hands clenched, turning the knuckles to the yellowish-white of a plucked fowl. 'Were you aware of anything unusual in his behaviour recently?'

Sheridan gave a harsh laugh. 'Unusual? I think Alexander was the most unusual man I've ever known.

Shrewd, mercurial, highly talented. Gifted with the soul of a poet, and a silver tongue.'

In spite of what seemed a wilful misunderstanding, de Silva forced himself to be patient. Sheridan was a difficult man to question but he must persist. 'I meant did he behave in a way that wasn't characteristic?'

There was a tap at the door. Clutterbuck called out and a servant entered. 'The government agent is on the telephone for you, sahib.'

Clutterbuck pushed back his chair and hauled himself to his feet. 'Tell him I'm on my way.' He turned to de Silva. 'I expect William Petrie wants an update. I'll try and keep it short.'

The door closed behind him. Sheridan hesitated briefly then leant forward. 'If you'd like to know who wanted Alexander dead, Inspector, the answer is simple: his wife and her lover, Paul Mayne. I'd advise you to take a very good look at them.'

De Silva frowned. 'If you're accusing them of murder, Mr Sheridan, that's a very serious allegation. Do you have anything to support it?'

'Oh, I have no actual proof, but who else stood to gain? It's been obvious for a long time that Mayne wants to take over the company. He was always jealous of Alexander. Alone, she would never have done anything, but she's under Mayne's spell.'

This was an interesting development. It was the first time it had been suggested that there was anything between Mayne and Kathleen Danforth. Maybe it was true. He thought of his meeting with Danforth and Emerald Watson. They had seemed very at home in each other's company. Had the Danforths' marriage been in trouble?

All the same, he reminded himself, motive wasn't everything; there must also be opportunity. Mayne's dressing room was at the opposite end of the theatre and, according to the caretaker, it was impossible to reach Danforth's from there without being seen. Kathleen Danforth however…

He heard footsteps in the corridor and braced himself for the reappearance of Archie Clutterbuck's bulky figure, but instead the same servant as before entered. 'The sahib is unable to come back today,' said the man. 'He says there is no need for you to wait, and arrangements have been made for the gentlemen to be driven back to their hotel.'

De Silva frowned. It wasn't particularly surprising that Petrie wanted an update, yet why did it have to disrupt the investigation? Briefly, he wondered if there was something else going on, but the thought didn't detain him for long. He was more bothered about the awkward situation Clutterbuck's high-handed manner put him in. If he continued the questioning, he would have to explain himself later. On the other hand, compliance made him look like a lackey. He hovered between the choices then, seeing the wry expression on Sheridan's face, made a swift decision.

'Tell them I'll follow them there.'

It should also provide an opportunity to search the bus.

CHAPTER 5

'Please come in and take a seat, Mr Raikes.'

The Nuala Hotel was a modest establishment, not nearly as grand as the Crown where Kathleen Danforth and Emerald Watson were staying, but the owner had been obliging and found de Silva a spare room where he could interview the remaining members of the company without attracting attention. It looked as if it hadn't been used for a while. The walls were drab and the wooden floor dusty, but it served the purpose.

A small table and two chairs stood in a corner to one side of the single window. Bert Raikes sat down opposite de Silva and pulled a green and gold tin of tobacco from his pocket. 'Mind if I smoke, Inspector?'

De Silva shook his head and waited while Raikes extracted a cigarette paper from a cloth pouch, added a few pinches of tobacco from the tin and proceeded to make his roll-up. From his leathery, nicotine-stained fingers, de Silva guessed it was one of many.

He looked to be in his late forties or early fifties, of middling height with broad shoulders and a bull neck. His grizzled hair was cut very close to his skull and his pale-blue eyes were set in a face that had a lived-in air. He also had what appeared to be recently sustained grazes on his hands. He finished his task, lit up and took the first puff. 'Terrible business the major going like that,' he said when he had exhaled a cloud of smoke. 'I still think of him as the major. I was his batman in the war. Old habits die hard.'

'How would you describe him?'

'A gentleman. The best officer you could wish to serve under. You'd have trouble finding anyone with a bad word to say about him. I know Frank Sheridan from those days too. He was a captain in the same battalion. Never got on with him all that well – he was difficult to fathom, everybody thought so. He was devoted to the major though. Not surprising, he would have been a goner if the major hadn't saved him from a Jerry sniper's bullet, but they couldn't be more different.'

He took another puff of the roll-up. 'The major was the life and soul of every party. Sheridan's a loner.'

'Are you aware of anyone who might have borne Mr Danforth a grudge?'

Raikes shook his head. 'As I say, everyone admired him.'

'Tell me more about Frank Sheridan. Did he join the company straight after the war?'

'Pretty much so. I heard he went to pieces for a while, then the major threw him a lifeline. I'm not sure exactly when it was though. I joined the company a few months later on.'

In other words, Sheridan had a powerful reason to be grateful to Alexander Danforth. If it was true that Paul Mayne and Kathleen Danforth were having an affair, Sheridan's loyalty to Danforth might influence his claim that they were responsible for his murder.

'What do you know about Mrs Danforth's relationship with her husband?'

Raikes raised an eyebrow. 'You know about her, do you? I suppose Sheridan told you. She and that bastard Mayne have been carrying on for months. He only got the job because she took a fancy to him and persuaded the major to hire him, but it doesn't mean anything. The major and she had an arrangement.' He gave a dry chuckle. 'Open marriage, she calls it. Bloody licence to act like a tart in my book, but there's women for you. If the major didn't object, who was I to? Anyway, he had his own fun.' He grinned. 'That pretty little Miss Watson's no better than she should be, and she wasn't the first to catch his eye.'

De Silva couldn't help feeling somewhat shocked. If Raikes had his facts straight, Alexander Danforth had truly been having an affair with a woman young enough to be his daughter.

'Are you a married man, Mr Raikes?'

Raikes' face darkened. 'Was. Ran off while I was away fighting in France, didn't she. Only found out after I was demobbed.'

'I'm sorry.'

'Long time ago. Water under the bridge.'

Still, unsurprising that he had a jaundiced view of the female sex, thought de Silva.

'The grazes on your hands, Mr Raikes. How did you come by them?'

Raikes scratched irritably at a red patch. 'Working on some new scenery. It's an occupational hazard. The only wood I can get in the market up here is sub-standard. It splinters easily.'

De Silva reached down and pulled the bag containing the scissors out of his holdall. There was always a chance that a murderer confronted with the fatal weapon might let his or her guard slip. Raikes, however, looked unmoved. De Silva guessed that his war service had left him less susceptible than most people.

'Do you recognise these, Mr Raikes?'

Raikes didn't answer at first, then, to de Silva's surprise, he saw that the man's eyes had filled with tears. Raikes sniffed and knuckled them away, then nodded. 'And I'd like to get my hands on the bastard who used them,' he muttered.

'Do you have any idea at all who that might be?'

Raikes leant forward, the tension in his body palpable. De Silva watched him, refraining from pressing for an answer. He wondered if the man would come out with the same accusation that Frank Sheridan had, but at last he shook his head. 'If I did, you'd be the first to know, but—'

His shoulders slumped and, suddenly, he looked ten years older. 'I can't understand it. It's hard to believe it was anyone in the company. Mayne's too cocksure for his own good but he's not got the guts.' He raised a disparaging eyebrow. 'When he first joined, he used to go green at the first drop of stage blood. Nah, he wouldn't do it. Sheridan was devoted to the major. Morville's a harmless bloke and Crichton's all talk. As for her...'

'Mrs Danforth?'

Raikes nodded. 'I can't believe she'd do it. Even if they did both stray sometimes, she and the major were fond of each other. Never mind what anyone tells you different. No, whoever killed him was from outside.'

De Silva sighed. In view of what the caretaker had told him, that seemed unlikely, but perhaps he needed to be more circumspect about taking the man's word at face value. That was something he must deal with later. For the present, he would continue with his interviews. Not everyone might share Raikes' conviction.

'Thank you for your help, Mr Raikes. If I have any more questions, I'll let you know. Would you ask Mr Morville to come and see me now, please?'

Gruffly, Raikes mumbled his assent. As he stood up, the sunshine filtering through the dusty window fell on his face. De Silva saw that, once more, his eyes were wet.

* * *

It took de Silva a moment to recognise that Morville was the actor who had played Ophelia's father, Polonius. He had obviously worn a wig on stage for instead of having white hair, he was nearly bald with mild, grey eyes. De Silva guessed that he was in his forties, about the same age as Frank Sheridan, but Morville looked more worn down, his gangly figure encased in beige trousers and a drab-green jacket, its too-short sleeves revealing bony wrists. He exuded a weary, mournful air that made it hard to credit he had the energy to murder anyone.

'I'd like to help, Inspector,' he said apologetically. 'But I'm afraid I haven't much to tell you. I was in my dressing room all afternoon, going over my lines and having a nap. I must admit to finding the heat in your country very overpowering. I went to the green room a little before six o'clock and I had no idea anything was wrong until Frank Sheridan came in.'

'Were you the last person to arrive in the green room?'

'Yes, the others were already assembled.'

'How did Mr Sheridan look when he raised the alarm?'

'Strange, even for him. He looked completely blank. It must have been the shock. But then Raikes asked him if he'd seen a ghost. Joking, of course, and that fired him up. If I hadn't grabbed his arm. I think he would have decked the poor fellow.'

'What about his clothes and hands? Was there any blood on them?'

'No. He said he hadn't touched the body. Raikes took charge after that and kept us all at a distance. He knew enough not to disturb the scene of a crime.'

De Silva made a note. 'How well did you know Mr Danforth?' he asked.

'I'd like to think we were good friends, although I hadn't known him for as long as Sheridan or Raikes had.'

'I understand they served together in the war.'

Morville looked away. 'The army's medical board turned me down. I had TB when I was a boy, so I spent the war pushing papers.'

'Pushing papers?'

'Deskwork. Nothing of any interest or importance.'

'How did you come to join the company?'

'I'd always had a yen to go on the stage as a career. I'd done plenty of amateur dramatics.' He smiled ruefully. 'Believe it or not, Inspector, I was considered quite good-looking when I was a young man. I haven't always played dodderers.'

Briefly, de Silva tried to imagine Morville as a young man. Yes, the high cheekbones and sad eyes, combined with what must have been slenderness in his youth, might well have made him a romantic figure. One of those poets who wandered lonely as a cloud over the green fields of England. He smiled. 'I'm sure you haven't, sir.'

'Anyway, not long after the war, I saw in *The Times* that applications were invited for a theatre group Alexander was setting up. I auditioned and was accepted and I haven't regretted it since, especially later on when Alexander decided to tour in warmer climes. The idea of seeing faraway places was very enticing and I thought the heat would be beneficial for my lungs too. Have you ever been to England, Inspector?'

De Silva shook his head.

'If you had, you'd know what I mean by a pea souper. A filthy mix of soot and fog that makes you choke, even if you have lungs of iron. When you have sponges like mine, it will eventually kill you.'

'What can you tell me about Mr Danforth? To the best of your knowledge, had he enemies?'

Morville shook his head. 'Alexander was the most charming of men. I've never come across anyone who didn't like him.'

'Were you aware of any money troubles he might have had?'

'Money troubles? Not that I know of. If Alexander was in debt, he kept it to himself, although I doubt the company made him rich. Don't misunderstand me, we've lived well and Alexander was always generous but I suspect he had more style than substance.'

'What can you tell me about Paul Mayne?' de Silva asked.

'Ah, our young Lothario. Kathleen Danforth likes to amuse herself with him but he's fundamentally harmless. The only person Mayne really loves is himself.'

'And you don't think her husband objected?'

'Actors are different, Inspector. A little judicious infidelity goes with the bohemian life. I'm sure Alexander always knew that Kathleen would send Mayne packing if he asked her to.'

De Silva frowned. This chimed with Bert Raikes' views, but he found such a casual attitude to marriage hard to comprehend. Was the fact that you spent your working hours pretending to be someone else really an excuse?

'What's your general opinion of Mrs Danforth?'

Morville pondered for a moment before answering. De Silva had already marked him down as a quiet but shrewd observer. 'You need to take care if you want to stay on the right side of her. She's temperamental and capricious and takes great offence if anyone dares to puncture the aura of youth and beauty she likes to project. Take this business with Paul Mayne for example. She needs to know she can still attract a much younger man. She's also difficult to work for. A lot of maids have come and gone over the years.'

'What about Olive Reilly? Has she been with her long?'

'About a year. She joined us in Calcutta. She comes from an army family and she'd been living there looking after her widowed mother who'd been an invalid for years. When the mother died, naturally the army pension died with her, and Olive needed a job. I think she may fare better with Kathleen than most of her predecessors, she's very capable and seems a tough nut.'

'But in spite of everything, do you believe that Mrs Danforth's prime loyalty was always to her husband?'

'Absolutely, and his to her, even though they'd both had, shall we say, other interests from time to time.' He rested his elbows on the table and pressed the tips of his fingers together. 'You're not convinced, Inspector.'

'It's too early to reach any conclusions, sir, but your colleague, Mr Sheridan, takes a different view of Paul Mayne.'

Morville sighed. 'Inspector, you need to understand that Frank Sheridan dislikes Paul Mayne intensely. Whereas the rest of us understand that if you don't want trouble, you have to be careful around Sheridan and leave him alone when he doesn't want to talk, Mayne taunts him. I know what Sheridan's been saying but the idea that Mayne is responsible for the outrage, with or without Kathleen's help, is preposterous. Mayne could no more manage the company on his own than fly, and he knows it. Sheridan's just a tricky customer. He seems to feel life hasn't treated him as it should and that makes him bitter.'

'What do you know about him?'

'Bert Raikes, who knows more about him than I do, once told me he came from a wealthy family, but he was the black sheep. Before the war, he had a variety of jobs, I believe. Playing piano in a nightclub and dabbling in antiques among them.'

'Has there ever been anything between him and Mrs Danforth?'

Morville threw back his head and laughed. 'Sheridan and Kathleen? He'd be far too complicated for her. Anyway, as I said, she likes her men younger. No, Frank has never had much luck with the ladies. Don't misunderstand me, I doubt there's anything of the other about him, if you know what I mean. I think he's just always been plain scared of anything in a skirt.'

He scratched his chin with a neatly clipped fingernail. 'Actually, there was a girl I think Sheridan might have been sweet on way back. At least, he was a bit more sociable than usual if she was around, not that that's saying much. But, if he was, it didn't come to anything. She was far keener on Alexander, like they all are. Women have always stuck to him like flies to paper. Apparently, she and Alexander had known each other from before the war and she joined the company about the same time as Sheridan. Now what was her name? Polly... Polly Devlin. That was it. She was very pretty – rather in the same style as our young Miss Watson, but the similarity's only skin deep. Emerald's a straightforward girl. Polly Devlin was anything but. Moody with a wild streak would describe her better. I always thought she was neurotic. Things cooled off between her and Alexander pretty quickly and after that, she left the company. Probably just as well really.'

De Silva rotated his pen between the forefinger and thumb of his right hand. He was beginning to despair of learning anything that would be useful in this investigation.

'Poor old Bert,' Morville went on. 'You may already know something of his history. He came back from the war to find his wife had left him and taken their kiddie too. The company's his life and God only knows what will happen to it with Alexander gone. Bert's the last person who would want him dead.'

Morville removed his elbows from the table and leant back in his chair. 'So, Inspector, if you were hoping I'd be able to give you any clues about who killed him, I'm afraid I must disappoint you, because I haven't the glimmer of an idea.'

De Silva shifted in his seat. The hotel would do well to consider purchasing more comfortable chairs.

'Thank you for your help all the same, Mr Morville,' he said civilly. 'Just one more thing.' He picked up the bag that still lay on the table and took out the scissors. 'Do you have any idea who these belong to?'

'I presume they're the ones that killed poor Alexander.'

'Yes, although their ownership isn't necessarily proof of guilt. They could have been stolen.'

Morville shrugged. 'Very true, but anyway I can't help you with that either.'

'What will you do now the company has lost its leader?'

'I'm not sure. I suppose it's best to wait for the dust to settle then see who's interested in carrying on. We'd need to find a new actor, possibly two, to fill Alexander's shoes, but we have plenty of bookings lined up. I've no desire to return to England. I've been gone too long.'

He half rose from his seat. 'If you have no further questions, Inspector?'

'Not at the moment. Thank you for your time.'

'Shall I ask one of the others to come in?'

De Silva nodded. 'Please.'

The door closed behind Morville and a few minutes passed before de Silva heard footsteps in the corridor. They were loud and brisk as if their owner was impatient. The door handle jerked down and, glowering, Paul Mayne made his entrance. His thick, coppery hair was untidy and his startling blue eyes flashed a challenge. Although he was probably in his late twenties, he gave the impression of a truculent schoolboy called to the headmaster's office.

De Silva stood up. 'Good afternoon, Mr Mayne, please take a seat.'

Mayne slumped into a chair. De Silva thought for a moment that it might collapse under the young man's tall, broad frame. 'I know what people are saying,' Mayne snarled.

'What would that be, sir?'

'That I killed Alexander Danforth.'

'And who are these people?'

'Sheridan. And I'd put money on it that it won't be long before he infects the rest of them.'

'And what have you to say?'

Mayne shifted in his chair, jolting the table. De Silva's pen rolled away and he caught it just before it went over the edge. Mayne scowled. 'The man's a maniac.'

'Putting the question of Mr Sheridan's state of mind aside, why would he single you out?'

'Because he dislikes me. Has done from the first and he's been even more difficult to get on with of late.' He gave a bark of laughter. 'For some obscure reason, Danforth had a soft spot for the malevolent crab. If it'd been up to anyone else, he would have been given his marching orders long ago.'

'I understand that Mr Sheridan thought very highly of Mr Danforth in return. Perhaps your relations with his wife coloured his view of you?'

Mayne flushed. 'Danforth only had himself to blame.'

'What do you mean by that?'

'He humiliated her. A woman like Kathleen won't put up with that for long. Emerald Watson was the latest conquest. The latest of many. I hoped it would at last convince Kathleen to leave him and I think she was on the verge of agreeing, but now…'

This wasn't the story de Silva had heard from Bert Raikes or Michael Morville. He wondered what the truth was.

'She's just called me to say it's over between us,' Mayne continued bitterly. 'Something about respect for his memory.'

De Silva studied the young man's baffled expression. Kathleen Danforth's reaction certainly didn't seem that of a woman who had inveigled her lover into killing her husband. Either the two of them played a clever game and

Mayne was lying, or, now that she was free, she wanted rid of him before he demanded more of her than the amusement of a romantic intrigue.

If Mayne had just been a toy, or a stick with which to goad Kathleen's husband, de Silva felt quite sorry for him. Unless he was putting on a very good act – and de Silva remembered he had been fairly wooden as Horatio in Hamlet – he was more likely to be a naïve, rather vain young man haplessly caught between two charming and unconventional people than a murderer.

As the sun moved westwards and ceased to warm the small room, he put a few more questions to Mayne but it was not with any hope of a great revelation. He claimed he had never seen the scissors before and de Silva rapidly formed the view that Morville and Raikes were right. Mayne didn't have much going for him except his good looks.

De Silva's thoughts drifted. He wondered how much longer Archie Clutterbuck would insist that Kathleen Danforth mustn't be troubled and how necessary his delicacy was. She was the only person, apart from her maid perhaps, who would have been able to go to her husband's dressing room without attracting attention. Her reaction to questioning might be the key that unlocked the mystery.

He came back to reality to find Paul Mayne fidgeting in his chair, watching him with a confused expression. De Silva blinked. 'My apologies, Mr Mayne. I had very little sleep last night. I think that will be all for now. I won't detain you any longer. Would you ask Mr Crichton to come in, please?'

In contrast to Michael Morville, Charles Crichton reminded de Silva of Dickens' Mr Pickwick. The robes of the King of Denmark had concealed a burly chest and fleshy thighs that were rendered all too apparent by modern dress. For a man who was probably in his mid-fifties, his face was surprisingly cherubic with plump cheeks and moist pink lips. He seemed more subdued than he had on the night of the murder; de Silva wondered why. Was it that the cold light of day had brought him to the realisation that his livelihood was now in doubt or was there something more to it?

In response to de Silva's invitation, Crichton sat down, the chair protesting faintly under his weight. De Silva noticed a strong aroma of whisky and remembered he had observed it the previous evening too. He turned to a fresh page in his notebook.

'I understand from your remarks last night that you had a high opinion of Alexander Danforth, sir. To the best of your knowledge, was there anyone in the company who didn't share that opinion?'

Crichton looked startled. 'Everyone admired him, Inspector. I can't imagine why you're asking.'

'Even Paul Mayne?'

'I meant everyone whose opinion was worth having.'

'And you don't number Mayne among them?'

'No. Mayne's a spoilt fool with an over-inflated idea of his own talent. It always surprised me that Danforth kept him on. I imagine Kathleen had a lot to do with that.'

'Do you think there was something between them?'

'I'm sure of it.'

'Have you been with the company long?'

'About ten years.'

'Then you knew Alexander Danforth pretty well?'

Crichton took a deep breath and for a moment de Silva was afraid he was about to be treated to another display of his thespian talents, but the broad chest deflated and de Silva realised that it was more likely that Crichton was attempting to master his emotions. Perhaps last night's more melodramatic personality corresponded with the amount the man had drunk.

Crichton looked away. 'I hope he counted me as a friend,' he said quietly. 'I certainly had a great regard for him.'

'What did you do before you joined the company, Mr Crichton?'

'I've always been an actor.' He waved a hand in an expansive gesture. 'As they say, acting is in my blood. I've shared a stage with some of the best in the business.'

De Silva remembered the menace the man had exuded in the role of King Claudius and had little difficulty believing it. Might he be using his acting skills to cover up something sinister?

'And what persuaded you to leave England?'

A wary look came into Crichton's eyes and he hesitated. 'I'll be honest with you, Inspector,' he said at last. 'My career was in danger of stalling – fashions change, you know. I was at the end of a long run in the West End and nothing was coming up except a few auditions for parts I wasn't confident I'd win. Money was getting tight, then I happened to meet Alexander and we hit it off.'

Another instance of the kindness of the man.

The sight of the scissors produced a shudder from Crichton but his vehement denial that he knew who owned them seemed genuine. De Silva asked a few more questions but learnt nothing useful.

When Crichton had gone, he closed his eyes and massaged the lids with his fingertips. His shoulders and neck ached. Not a very auspicious start; getting to the bottom of this wasn't going to be easy.

He went to see the hotel manager and asked where the company's bus was parked. Taken to a large shed behind the hotel, fortunately, he found the vehicle unlocked. He spent some time on his search but it revealed nothing of interest. He hoped he wouldn't have cause to regret the delay.

When he had thanked the manager for his help, he returned to the police station. A message from Archie

Clutterbuck awaited him, telling him that on no account was he to speak with Kathleen Danforth or Emerald Watson until further notice.

Jane was out for the evening at one of Florence Clutterbuck's soirées so he wasn't in any particular hurry to go home. Instead, he settled down at his desk and wrote up the notes he had made that afternoon, embellishing them with his thoughts. When he reached the end, he frowned. He wasn't very satisfied with the result but there was nothing more to be done tonight. Tucking the pages in one of his desk drawers, he locked it and pocketed the key.

Dusk approached swiftly as he drove home. By the time he arrived, it was dark. Lights flared in the bungalow's windows, but he delayed going inside for a while to take a turn around the garden.

The moon hung low on the horizon; liquorice shadows dappled the grass. Here and there in the flowerbeds, gleams of silver highlighted stems and leaves. He stopped beside his cherished roses. Next month, it would be time to prune them. He always liked to see the plants trimmed and sheared of last season's crisped and mottled leaves. It heralded the time when they would bloom again in all their crimson, pink, and primrose glory.

The scent of hibiscus wafted towards him as he reached the trellised archway that divided the flower garden from his vegetable plot. Beyond it, shining trails meandered across the path. His eyes followed them to a bed of cabbage stumps where a dozen or so slugs and snails were enjoying a leisurely feast. Sluggish: the word settled in his mind like an overly rich meal on a sweltering day. Sluggish defined exactly how he felt. It was never a good thing when the way ahead was strewn with obstacles. He wondered again how long he would have to wait before he was able to interview Kathleen Danforth. Surely Archie Clutterbuck must agree to it soon?

His chin jutted and he took a deep breath. There was no use getting frustrated. He must do something to distract himself. Going over to the nearby shed, he found a tin bucket and some old gloves. Jane would tell him off for doing a job the gardeners were supposed to carry out but some garden chores were therapeutic.

One by one, he collected the slugs and snails and dropped them in the bucket then crossed the garden and deposited them carefully in a patch of uncultivated ground. Some people said you should kill them with salt but the idea offended his Buddhist principles. Didn't snails and slugs have as much right to live as anything else? He didn't grudge it them provided they left his vegetables in peace.

He remembered the words Jane had told him for groups of slugs and snails: a cornucopia of slugs and a walk of snails. English was a marvellously expressive language – parliaments of rooks, conspiracies of ravens, murders of crows.

Murder: there it was again. There was no escape from his predicament.

He took the bucket back to the shed, removed the gloves, and then wiped his hands on a piece of sacking that hung from a nail by the door. He would wash his hands properly in the house.

The moon was higher now, hanging in the clear sky like a dented silver coin. He breathed in the cooling night air and thought of dinner. He wasn't fond of eating alone – food tasted best in good company – but he had missed lunch and he was hungry. Perhaps after he had eaten, he would read some more of Shakespeare's sonnets.

CHAPTER 6

He slept more soundly than he expected and woke refreshed, feeling less gloomy about the challenges that awaited him. Jane was already up and he found her in the dining room having breakfast.

'You must have been tired, dear,' she said, smiling. 'You didn't wake when I came in, or when I got up this morning.'

'I expect I needed to catch up on the sleep I lost the other night.'

He sat down and took a piece of toast from the toast rack.

'That will be cold. Wait for one of the servants to bring some more.' Jane rang the little brass bell beside her cup and saucer.

'It's alright, I'm hungry. I'll eat this piece while I wait.'

He began to spread butter liberally. 'How was your evening?'

'Oh, very entertaining. Florence arranged a pleasant supper, although it wasn't one you would have enjoyed all that much. We had creamed tomato soup followed by roast lamb and mint sauce, then rice pudding.'

De Silva chuckled. 'Sturdy British food.'

'And very filling.' Jane patted her midriff. 'I'm only having a light breakfast.' She indicated the neatly sliced mango on her plate. De Silva sniffed appreciatively at the sweet, honeyed aroma.

A servant entered and Jane ordered more toast. 'And two poached eggs for me,' de Silva added. He smiled at Jane. 'I think I'll have a light breakfast too. No curry today.'

The servant bustled off. 'Now,' said Jane as the door closed, 'I'm longing to know what you've found out about poor Mr Danforth's murder.'

'Not nearly as much as I would like. So far, I've interviewed the men in the company but Archie still hasn't agreed to my seeing Mrs Danforth or Miss Watson.'

'Why ever not?'

He shrugged. 'I've no idea. It's as if he deliberately wants to obstruct the investigation.'

Jane forked up a slice of mango. 'On the other hand, it is less than two days since it happened. Mrs Danforth must still be very shocked and Emerald Watson is so young. I saw Peggy Appleby last night and she says she's terribly distressed. Peggy has become quite a good friend of hers, you know. The Applebys were one of the couples from the Amateur Dramatic Society who helped with the production of Hamlet.'

De Silva forbore to mention that there might be a more specific reason for Emerald Watson's distress, but he hadn't reckoned with Jane's sharp eye.

'Is there something you're not telling me?'

'One thing I've been told is that she and Alexander Danforth were having an affair.'

'Gracious me! But she's so much younger than he was, and right under his wife's nose too?'

'Apparently.'

Jane finished her mango and pushed away the plate. 'True or not, I hope the story doesn't go any further. Mrs Danforth has just lost her husband and it would be unforgiveable to add to her misery.'

She broke off as the servant reappeared with the eggs and toast and set them down in front of de Silva.

'But then,' he said when the servant had departed, 'if one believes it, Kathleen Danforth was also having an affair. It seems the Danforths were fundamentally happy together, but had an unconventional attitude to marriage and both of them turned a blind eye when the other strayed.'

'You say *if* one believes it.'

'You've hit on the crux of the matter.'

Jane listened carefully as he expanded on what he had been told. 'You're right, of course,' she said with a frown when he had finished. 'If Mrs Danforth wasn't as forgiving of her husband's behaviour as you've been led to believe, jealousy would be a powerful motive. Even if she was unfaithful herself, she might have thought her husband's affair was more of a threat this time. But all the same, it's horrible to think she would get this man Mayne to kill him.'

'If I remember rightly, you were of the opinion that scissors are a woman's weapon. You also pointed out that feminine scruples didn't deter Lady Macbeth from urging her husband to commit murder.'

'Yes, I know.' She shivered. 'But I wasn't being entirely serious. You don't really think that it's true, do you?'

'I think it's questionable. Bert Raikes − he's not one of the actors, he does odd jobs and makes scenery − told me he's seen Mayne turn green at the sight of stage blood, so it's doubtful he could cope with the real thing. Secondly, Mayne's dressing room is at the opposite end of the theatre to Alexander Danforth's. If the caretaker I spoke with is correct, no one can go between the two sides without passing his booth, and he insists that no one did at the time in question. He also told me that when there is no performance, anyone entering the theatre has to come in through the stage door and he would see them.' He paused. 'Kathleen Danforth's dressing room, however, is on the same side of the theatre as her husband's.'

Jane frowned. 'That means she had the opportunity to

commit the murder, but would she have the strength to overpower him?'

'It seems unlikely, but I'm waiting to find out whether Danforth was drugged before he was stabbed.'

Jane shivered again. 'It's a horrible thought. Let's suppose for now that Sheridan is wrong, and consider the rest of the company. What about Sheridan himself?'

'He's the one who found Danforth's body. According to Raikes, and Sheridan's own statement, he was very close to Danforth. There doesn't seem to be any benefit to him from Danforth's death, in fact quite the reverse. He told me, and Raikes corroborated it, that Danforth saved his life in the war. Raikes also told me that Sheridan was in very bad shape after it and Danforth helped him out. Sheridan's an abrasive character too. Not the kind of man to make a success of the company on his own.'

'That might not stop him from trying. Could he have gone to the dressing room without being spotted?'

'No, for the same reason as Mayne. Then there's Morville, the actor who played Ophelia's father, Polonius, but he has no discernible motive and the situation is the same with his dressing room. That goes for Bert Raikes too and he gives the impression of having been devoted to Danforth.'

He mopped up a puddle of egg yolk with some toast.

'Charles Crichton, who played King Claudius, was the last of the men I interviewed, and I'd guess the oldest by quite a few years. I think he may have an alcohol problem. Both yesterday and this morning, there was a strong smell of whisky about him. Off the top of my head, I don't see how he would benefit from Danforth's death. According to Crichton, the first time they met was when he auditioned for a place in the company. If that's the case, there would be no past history where they might have fallen out. He admitted that before he joined Danforth, his career was going badly so one would think he'd look on Danforth as a good man who gave him a helping hand.'

'Danforth seems to have made a habit of extending helping hands.'

'Yes, he did. If we discount the allegation about his wife and Paul Mayne, it's difficult to see who would want him out of the way. And even if we thought there was a motive, we have the problem of opportunity with all of the men. Unless the caretaker is lying, none of them could have entered Danforth's dressing room between four o'clock and just before six, the time when Sheridan found the body, without being noticed.'

'Are you sure Sheridan didn't have time to kill Danforth then raise the alarm?'

'He was only gone from the green room for a few moments. Anyway, Morville confirmed there was no blood on Sheridan's clothes or hands. It would have been impossible for him to attack Danforth without getting blood on himself.'

'That does present a problem.'

'Yes. And even if there had been time to change into clean clothes, what did he do with the bloodstained ones? I searched the dressing rooms and found nothing.'

'The maid?'

'Unlikely. She hasn't been with the company for long and there's no evidence she knew any of them previously. She was down on her luck when she joined. Her invalid mother who she'd looked after for years had died leaving her alone in Calcutta with no money. Presumably she still needs the job so it would be in her interest for Danforth to be alive and the company to continue functioning successfully.'

He paused. 'Finally, we have Emerald Watson.'

'But she seems such a sweet girl. Not a murderess by any stretch of the imagination, and she may have been in love with him.'

'Appearances can be deceptive. All the same, she too would have to pass the caretaker to get to Danforth's dressing room.'

'So, they were in the green room shortly before the dress rehearsal was due to start,' said Jane, half to herself. 'Danforth didn't appear and Sheridan went to fetch him; found him dead and raised the alarm.'

She pondered for a few moments then clapped her hands. 'I have the answer! They were all in it together, just like the plot in Mrs Christie's novel that came out a couple of years ago. It was about a murder on the Orient Express. The victim was an American tycoon called Ratchett. He was found dead in his compartment, stabbed twelve times. Hercule Poirot happened to be travelling on the train so he was asked to take over the investigation.'

'And what did those famous little grey cells discover?'

'Years before, under another name, Ratchett had kidnapped the young daughter of a wealthy family and demanded a ransom. The family paid, but he killed the poor child anyway. There were lots of clues and red herrings that led you to suspect different people in turn but, eventually, Poirot came to the conclusion that there were two solutions.'

'And they were?'

'All the passengers and staff were still on the train. The window in Ratchett's compartment was open when his body was found, so the murderer might have been a stranger who escaped that way. The problem with *that* was that, due to an avalanche, the train was stuck in a snowdrift and there were no footprints in the snow.'

'Hmm. Wind might have blown a fresh drift over them.'

'Perhaps, but Poirot thought it more likely the murderer was still on the train. In the end he offered a second solution. It was that Ratchett's fellow passengers had all been connected with the little girl and conspired to take revenge for her death. One of the passengers admitted to Poirot that was the truth.'

'What happened in the end?'

'He suggested to the director of the railway company that when the police arrived, they should be told the first version to protect the bereaved family and the director agreed.'

De Silva nodded. 'A fitting outcome, even if not exactly within the law.'

'I thought so.'

He smiled teasingly. 'One problem with this ingenious theory is that there was only one stab wound on Danforth's body.'

'Then one of them struck the blow and the rest are protecting him.'

The depressing thought occurred to de Silva that if Jane had hit on the truth, it had been a mistake to delay searching the bus. Using it to return to their hotel, the members of the company might easily have removed evidence and disposed of it straight away.

No, surely this couldn't be a case where life mirrored art any more than it already had. Those words written in blood on the mirror were enough.

'Appealing as your solution is,' he said resolutely, 'it's hard to see all the members of the company having a common purpose and that being to kill Danforth.'

Jane sighed. 'Oh, very well, I give in. There are no obvious leads.'

'I'm afraid not.'

'What will you do next?'

'Finish my breakfast and read the paper for a while. I need a little respite from all this.'

Jane rolled her eyes. 'And after that?'

'I'll get in touch with Archie Clutterbuck. If I can't speak to him in person, I'll have to send a message.'

He crunched his last fragment of toast and wiped a sticky speck of orange marmalade from the corner of his mouth. 'I must press him for an answer about interviewing Mrs Danforth and Emerald Watson.'

He stood up and came round to Jane's side of the table to kiss her cheek.

'You'll be busy,' she said with a smile. 'I do hope Archie won't be too difficult.'

'So do I, my love.'

CHAPTER 7

At the station, he found Nadar on his own, doggedly typing up a report. The constable's typing was of the two-finger variety and de Silva was frequently grateful to the man who had invented the noiseless typewriter. A muffled clunk was infinitely easier to ignore than an insistent clack.

He gave Nadar the job of putting a call through to the Residence for an appointment with Clutterbuck, then retired to his office. A few minutes later, the constable tapped on the door and came in.

'I'm sorry, sir. They say Mr Clutterbuck is out and they're not sure what time he'll be back. I've left a message that you would like to see him.'

'Well done, Constable.'

Nadar hesitated.

'Yes?'

'Have you any leads yet, sir? I'd like to be more involved in the investigation if that's possible. It's… well, the whole town's talking about it. People keep asking me what's going on and saying I must know more than I'm telling.'

'And you'd like that to be true?'

Nadar flushed slightly. 'I suppose I would, sir.' He gave de Silva a sheepish smile. 'I hope I haven't spoken out of turn, sir.'

De Silva leant back in his chair. 'Remind me how old you are now, Constable.'

'Twenty-three, sir.' He drew himself up to his full height. 'As you know, sir, I am a family man. I want to advance in my work and do my best for them. I think I can do it.'

De Silva felt a twinge of self-reproach. Nadar was a conscientious young man, but it was easy to overlook him in favour of Sergeant Prasanna who gave the impression of having more pep. A good senior officer, however, ought to give all his staff a chance to shine.

He smiled at Nadar. 'Ambition is always laudable, young man. As long as you are prepared to put in the hard work that leads to success.'

'Oh, I am, sir.' Nadar's round face was a study in solemnity.

'I'm glad to hear it. I'll bear this conversation in mind.'

'Thank you, sir.'

He hesitated once more.

'Is there something else?'

'I was wondering if there's anything I can do straight away, sir.'

'Not for the moment, but I won't forget.'

'Very good, sir.'

When Nadar had gone, hopefully not discouraged, de Silva stood up and went to the window. Outside, the morning bustle was giving way to the quieter activity of the midday heat. His view of the bazaar showed stallholders lounging in the shade under limp awnings. At the nearest fruit stall, a few tardy shoppers browsed, inspecting the remaining offerings of mangoes, rambutans, pineapples, dragon fruit, and tamarinds before deciding whether to add more to the contents of their baskets.

He thought back to his childhood. His father had loved their garden even though, home being Colombo, it had been small compared with the one he had now at Sunnybank. In spite of that, his father had grown many kinds of fruit and vegetables. He closed his eyes and recalled the soft, creamy, seed-speckled flesh of the scarlet dragon fruits with their subtle sweetness. They had been his favourites, closely followed by the tangy pineapples.

His parents' cook had let him help to make some of the teas, juices, and preserves that could be prepared from the fruits. He had liked it best when they made wood apple jam. His job had been to smash the apples against the garden wall to get to the pulp inside the tough brown shells. The aroma released by this satisfying procedure was very like coffee. Raw, the sweet-sour taste of the pulp had made the inside of his mouth pucker, but boiled up into jam, it was delicious. The cook at Sunnybank still made it according to the family recipe.

The clock on the post office tower glinted in the sunshine as the hands crept towards lunchtime. His stomach rumbled but he hesitated to go home in case Clutterbuck telephoned. Perhaps he would send Nadar out to fetch him something. In view of their conversation this morning, it might be considerate to reassure him that being sent on the errand had nothing to do with his abilities, or lack of them.

Later, as he ate, he ran over what he had unearthed so far and wished it wasn't so unpromising. He only hoped that the way forward would be clearer once he had spoken to Emerald Watson and Kathleen Danforth.

His thoughts returned to the words written on the mirror in Danforth's blood: *the rest is silence*. He had checked and Jane was right, they were the last words Hamlet spoke before dying. By then, he knew he had accomplished the task of avenging his father that it had taken him the whole play to confront.

Was there a clue there? The fact that the words were a quotation might indicate that whoever wrote them was an actor, but that wasn't necessarily the case. Anyone who knew the play might remember them. Did the play hold the answer or was it just a distraction? Whatever the situation, he needed a stroke of luck, and he wasn't sure where it was coming from.

* * *

Lunch over, he indulged in his customary nap – after all, how was the brain to function properly if the digestion was not treated with respect? He was absolutely sure that Jane's beloved Monsieur Poirot would never have let a case interfere with the needs of the inner man.

Fifteen minutes did the trick and he returned to consciousness reinvigorated. Picking up a pen, he started on a letter to Archie Clutterbuck. He decided to keep it simple and confine himself to asking about when he might interview Kathleen Danforth and Emerald Watson. He would send his report on the information he had gleaned from the men later. It was always hard to know how Clutterbuck would take things, particularly where his instructions hadn't been followed to the letter. Best to read the signs before one spoke. Rushing in was like approaching an angry elephant without a handy tree nearby.

He read the letter over and sealed it up. This time, he didn't ring the bell for Nadar but went to the outer office and handed the envelope to him.

'Do you have your bicycle here?'

'Yes, sir.'

'Then please cycle up to the Residence and deliver this. After that, join me at the theatre.'

'Right, sir.'

'Where's Sergeant Prasanna, by the way?'

'He came in for a short time only, sir, then went home again. We did not like to disturb you, so he asked me to say that he hoped you would not mind. His wife is unwell. He will be sure to be back in the morning.'

De Silva frowned. He and Jane had become very fond of Kuveni when she lived with them before her marriage.

'I hope it's nothing serious?'

'I don't think so, sir, but he was worried.'

'Never mind, I'm sure you'll manage very well without him, Constable.'

Was he imagining it, or did Nadar's chest swell as he nodded?

* * *

A wave of trapped heat rolled out and engulfed him as he opened the driver's door of the Morris. He gave an exasperated snort; he must have been very distracted when he arrived this morning or he would have taken more care to park in the shade. With a grimace, he climbed in and wound down the window before closing the door. It wouldn't be so bad when he managed to get up a bit of speed. The road that led to the theatre should be fairly quiet at this time of day and it was lined with trees.

The breeze generated by the moving car soon cooled him but another problem arose. Perhaps the food Nadar had fetched for him hadn't been the freshest. A sharp pain stabbed him in the stomach and he flinched. He hoped the discomfort wouldn't get any worse. It was hard to maintain an air of gravitas when all you could think about was the whereabouts of the nearest toilet.

He balanced the steering wheel with one hand and leant across to reach the glove box. If he remembered correctly, there was a bottle of stomach pills there. The twisting movement increased the pain and, as he fumbled in the dark recess, he inhaled sharply. At last, his fingers closed on a small bottle that rattled when he shook it. Good, there they were.

He was just extracting the bottle when a loud blast from a horn made him jump; the bottle bounced into the footwell on the passenger side. De Silva's heart thumped as a sleek black car passed, its wing mirror almost grazing the Morris's. The Residence's chauffeur threw him a scowl. Occupied with recovering his composure and bringing the Morris back to its own side of the road, he just managed a brief glance to see who the passengers were. He was almost certain that one of them was Archie Clutterbuck.

Still shaken, he left the bottle of pills where it was and continued cautiously. The road he was on led not only to the theatre but also to the Residence. If Clutterbuck had been coming the other way, he must have been to one of them. If it was the Residence, why did the servant Nadar had spoken to say that his master was not at home? If it was the theatre, what had Clutterbuck been up to?

At the theatre, he parked the Morris at the back. The only other vehicle was a rusty bicycle that he presumed belonged to the caretaker. As he walked over to the stage door, he noticed it stood ajar. He pushed it a little further open and it emitted a creak of protest. Pausing on the threshold, he waited to see if the caretaker would notice he had a visitor, but only the hum of insects disturbed the silence.

He went in and, with his eyes not fully adjusted to the dim light after the brightness outside, bumped into a stack of wooden boxes that had been left there. Cursing under his breath, he rubbed his shins.

The caretaker was once again in his booth filling in a puzzle, but he stopped and looked up.

'This is a crime scene,' de Silva said testily, his shins still smarting. 'You need to keep the door closed or anyone might wander in.'

'I am sorry, sahib.' The man didn't look particularly apologetic. 'The fans do not work. If the doors and windows are shut, it is too hot to breathe. Everything here is old and run-down. Now there will be bad karma too.' A disgruntled expression settled on his face.

De Silva didn't comment. Unfortunately, it was highly probable that Danforth's murder would taint the theatre, at least until the memory of it faded, and, given the fact that life in Nuala was normally a placid affair, that would take a long time. It was no wonder the caretaker was discontented. Doubtless his job was badly paid. If the theatre fell into disuse, he would also lose the chance to boost his income by offering little extra services to companies who came to perform. Still, none of that was his problem and it was time he got down to business.

'Has anyone else been here today?' he asked.

The caretaker shook his head.

'You're certain of that?'

The man adopted an injured expression. 'I am always here, sahib.' A crafty look came into his eyes. 'Even though the wages are not enough to feed a dog.'

De Silva didn't rise to the bait. He'd heard of too many colleagues compromising themselves by going down that avenue. 'You should speak to your employer about that. For now, just remember the law requires you to answer my questions truthfully.'

The man glowered and muttered his assent.

Glancing around his booth, de Silva noticed a key rack attached to the wall. From it hung various keys. Some were so rusty that he doubted they had been used for years. Through a door, he glimpsed a room little bigger than a cubby hole that contained a low, unmade bed. On the floor beside it were a Calor gas ring, a chipped white enamel kettle and a tin plate and mug. A washing bowl with a dirty towel draped over one side completed the furnishings.

'Do you live here all the time?' he asked.

The caretaker nodded. 'The owner is afraid that thieves will break in if no one is here to guard it. Usually, I am on my own but most afternoons old Prathiv comes to talk and chew betel. He is lonely, but the owner says he is too old to work here now.'

De Silva wondered if Prathiv would be a less satisfactory employee than this man who did not appear to be doing very much. From what he had seen so far, he preferred his puzzles to cleaning and maintenance work.

The door creaked again and the sound of a thud came from the lobby, followed by a muffled howl. The boxes. A few seconds later, Nadar limped into view.

'Alright, Constable?'

'Yes, sir,' Nadar said valiantly.

The caretaker stiffened perceptibly at the sight of the young man. De Silva made a mental note to ask Nadar when they were alone what that was all about.

They left the caretaker to his puzzles and went their different ways in the theatre to make another search. 'It was late when I carried out my first one,' said de Silva. 'I want to be sure I didn't miss anything.'

After two hours, de Silva wearied and went to find Nadar. On the way, he remembered the question he'd wanted to ask his constable.

Nadar hesitated. 'Before I was a family man, sir,' he said at last, 'I sometimes went to one of the bars in town. People came to drink arrack but some also to gamble.' He stared at his feet.

'We were all young once, Nadar,' de Silva said cheerfully. 'Go on. I'm hoping that your misspent youth will be the key to an important discovery.'

Nadar grinned. 'This man was one of them. A very boastful fellow. He often talked about the easy job he had but he would not say what it was.'

Unsurprising, thought de Silva. He wouldn't want word to get around and cause him to lose it.

'I noticed his reaction. Clearly, he recognised you.'

'But he may not be sure from where, sir. I usually stayed in the background. And I never gambled,' he added quickly.

'I'm glad to hear it.'

De Silva weighed up this new piece of information. 'When you have time, Nadar, I'd like you to see what you can find out about this man's current habits. If he's lying about always being at his post, he could be careless about locking up when he leaves the theatre. Someone from outside the company could have engineered a way of getting in unnoticed and hidden somewhere. It might not necessarily be anyone who knew Danforth. It's a very long shot but a new theatre company occupying the place could tempt someone looking for easy pickings. We shouldn't yet discount the possibility that the murder was carried out in the course of a robbery. I'd like to go back to the dressing room and test how stout that door is. See if it's at all credible that Danforth was attacked by someone from outside – either an enemy or a burglar – and no one heard the noise.'

On the threshold of the dressing room, they both studied the door. De Silva ran his hand over the wood approvingly. 'It's a sturdy piece of wood and well made.' He glanced at the window on the wall opposite the dressing table then went over and looked out. 'It's not far to the ground, although it is visible from the road. But it's not beyond the bounds of possibility that someone climbed in this way.'

'Wouldn't Mr Danforth see them in the mirror as they approached him?'

'If he was conscious, one would think so, Constable.'

He stepped away from the entrance. 'Go inside and close the door, wait a minute or two then make some noise. I'll go to Mrs Danforth's dressing room and see if I can hear you.'

Nadar looked bemused. 'How shall I do that, sir?'

'Goodness, I don't know, lad. Use your imagination. Act as you would if someone was attacking you.'

Sitting in Kathleen Danforth's dressing room, de Silva listened intently. At first, all he heard was silence, then a string of bloodcurdling yells reached his ears. Chuckling, he followed the sounds back to Alexander Danforth's dressing room. When he opened the door, catching Nadar in full flow, he nodded. 'Very good, Constable, I'm sure you have a great future ahead of you if you decide to take to the stage.'

Nadar beamed. 'Thank you, sir. It was easier than I expected.'

'Well, whatever the lab comes up with, I think we can safely say that either the deceased knew his killer and trusted him, or he was drugged. No one would present their back to an interloper and, after your excellent performance, we can be sure that a struggle would have been audible.'

'If there was anyone in the other room to hear it, sir.'

De Silva frowned. 'Do you mean it might have been Mrs Danforth who killed her husband?'

An uneasy expression came over Nadar's face. 'I'm sorry, sir. It was foolish of me to suggest such a thing.'

'No, not at all, and you're not the first.'

Nadar brightened.

'I'm open to considering anyone as a suspect. There's a maid too; her name's Olive Reilly. I'd like to know where she was that night. I shall have to insist on cooperation from Mr Clutterbuck now. It's high time we were given the chance to question the ladies.'

'Yes, sir.'

Nadar looked impressed and de Silva felt a glow of pride at his own decisiveness.

CHAPTER 8

'But there are still many possibilities,' he said with a sigh. 'And I must admit, they have me flummoxed.'

He swallowed a mouthful of his after-dinner coffee.

Jane gave him a sympathetic smile. 'It's early days yet, dear. Don't be despondent, that's not like you.'

'I would be less so if Archie was more helpful.'

'It is strange he's not. Gallantry is all very well, but surely he understands that if you're to do your job, you need to question everyone.'

'One would think so.' He smiled ruefully. 'I told young Nadar that I was going to be firm but saying that is one thing and doing it another. I know from experience that dealing with Archie when he's in one of his stubborn moods is like trying to teach a bull elephant to dance.'

He finished his coffee. 'Anyway, the caretaker says his predecessor comes to the theatre most afternoons so I'll go back tomorrow.'

* * *

The following afternoon, he paused at the entrance to the theatre lobby, hearing the rattle of a dice shaker. The caretaker and his retired counterpart were so bent on their game that they didn't notice him at first. He watched the older man make his throw then, grinning widely to display a mouth sparsely furnished with betel-stained teeth, punch the air with a bony fist. Muttering, the caretaker pushed a few coins from the small pile at his elbow across the table.

De Silva cleared his throat and both men looked up. The caretaker rearranged his face in an ingratiating smile. 'This is Prathiv who I told you about, sahib.'

The old man, still grinning, climbed stiffly to his feet.

'Your friend tells me that you know the theatre better than anyone.'

Prathiv nodded. 'Fifty years I worked here, from when I was a young man.'

'Excellent, you're just the person I need.'

'What do you want to know, sahib?'

'Is there a way of getting from the dressing rooms down that corridor – he pointed to the one on the right – and the ones on the opposite side without passing by here?'

Prathiv thought for a while. 'Perhaps up in the rafters above the stage,' he said at last. 'There is a way across. There are ropes and pulleys there for when scenery needs to be pulled up or down. The British call it the flies.'

'How do you get there?'

'Above those dressing rooms.' He pointed to the right-hand corridor.

De Silva wondered why he hadn't noticed anything in his search. 'Can you show me?'

'Yes, sahib.'

'No one has used it since I have worked here,' cut in the caretaker. 'The roof leaks when the monsoon comes. The beams must be rotten by now.'

'I will show the sahib all the same.' Old Prathiv scowled at his friend. 'It will interest him.'

De Silva nodded. 'If it helps my investigation, I'll be grateful.'

'It will, sahib. I am sure of that.'

The caretaker shrugged.

Following the old man up increasingly narrow flights of stairs, de Silva wasn't surprised he hadn't gone through this door earlier. Its handle was so hard to turn that he recalled thinking it was locked. Silently, he ticked himself off for not being more persistent. However, when they finally reached the place, he decided that the lapse was immaterial. He should have taken the caretaker's word for it. No one would have used this route to reach Danforth's room. There was a strong smell of damp and, although winching tackle and the remains of a tattered backdrop still dangled from the beams, much of the wood was like honeycomb. Clearly, the theatre's recent refurbishment had been cosmetic only. There was also a blank wall at the far side. Without a very long ladder, descending to the stage would be extremely perilous.

He was about to say something sharp to the old man about dragging him up there for nothing but the words died as he looked down. His head swam; cautiously, he backed away and waited for the wobble in his knees to subside.

'Nothing that helps me there,' he said, hoping his discomfiture hadn't been obvious. 'Are there any other possibilities? I mean real ones,' he added sternly.

'There are passages to the cellar from both sides of the theatre.'

'It would have been better to have showed me those first.'

Prathiv looked disgruntled. No doubt he had hoped for a tip after all those stairs. On the slow descent to the ground floor, he hobbled along painfully, making a great performance of sighing and leaning on his stick. De Silva didn't feel too sorry for him.

The caretaker grinned when he saw them, probably guessing from Prathiv's sour expression that there had been no reward for his climb. A small vengeance for the defeat in the game of dice.

'They also have not been used for a long time,' he said dismissively when de Silva asked about the newly revealed passages. 'The ceilings are collapsed in many places. The sahib will have seen that there are doors with no handles on both the dressing room corridors. That is because the cellar passages they lead to are dangerous and no longer used.'

There was more muttering from Prathiv.

De Silva remembered noticing the doors and making a mental note to find out about them, but it didn't sound as if they were relevant anyway.

'Anything else either of you can tell me?' he asked. 'Are there any other ways to get into the cellar?'

The caretaker nodded. 'There is a door you can use, sahib, but only one. He scanned the rack of keys and selected a large one hanging from a rusty iron ring. 'This one fits it. If you wish, I will show you.'

De Silva frowned. How many other corridors and doors were there in this rabbit warren and why did he have to prise information from these people like oysters from a shell?

Outside, they followed a wall overgrown with creepers and scrub until they reached a place where the vegetation had been cleared a little to leave space around a door. The caretaker put the key in the lock and turned it with some difficulty. It looked as if it wasn't often used. The door opened to reveal a bare yard surrounded by high walls. De Silva noted it was on the same side of the building as the men's and Miss Watson's dressing rooms. There was a narrow window high up in one wall, but it looked impossible to reach. The door on the far side of the yard wasn't locked.

'What's the cellar used for?' de Silva asked as they went inside and the caretaker switched on a dim light.

'Scenery and costumes used to be stored here, but now it is too damp.'

There seemed to be a lot about this theatre that had been allowed to deteriorate, thought de Silva. A great pity Danforth's venture had ended so tragically. It might have been the spur that reversed the decline.

He went over to an odd, square contraption. It had a sinister air to it, as if it were a cage to imprison some terrified wretch in a dark dungeon, or a medieval instrument of torture. 'What's this?' he asked, eyeing it warily.

'The stage trap, sahib,' said the caretaker.

De Silva studied the assemblage of wood and metal with all its chains and weights. So this was what the mechanics from Gopallawa Motors had needed to fix so that the ghost of Hamlet's father could make its spectral entrance from the nether regions. He looked more closely and noticed that there were a couple of bent struts and other signs of recent damage. Perhaps it was fortunate that the machine had only needed to be used once. The repairs didn't look as if they were holding too well.

The caretaker grunted. 'Bad work,' he said sourly. Obviously, he was no fan of Gopallawa's mechanics. Perhaps the feeling was mutual.

'Did you bring the mechanics who mended this down here by the same route we came by just now?' he asked.

'Yes, sahib.'

'How many people are needed to operate the machine?'

'It is best with two, but one man can do it alone if necessary.'

'Who worked it on the evening of the performance?'

'I did, sahib, with Sahib Raikes.'

'Has anyone else been down to look at it?'

'The one with the thin face who does not speak.'

Ah, Sheridan again, but then he had played the ghost of Hamlet's father, so it would be natural to want to familiarise himself with the contraption in advance. He cast around for anything else worth asking. 'Would it be possible for anyone to operate it and go up on stage by themselves?'

Prathiv cackled and said something to the caretaker in rapid Tamil. De Silva didn't catch all the words but he understood enough to know that the remark would have been highly unsuitable if ladies had been present.

The caretaker stifled a laugh. 'It would not be safe at all, sahib, but maybe possible.'

Perhaps he could rule out the murderer making use of that route unless he or she had help, quite apart from the problem of getting down to the cellar in the first place.

The dank air didn't invite him to linger, but he wanted to be thorough. 'Before we go, you'd better show me this end of the passages we were talking about earlier,' he said.

It didn't take many minutes to establish that, even if the doors on the dressing room corridors were brought back into use, neither of the passages would have been passable without moving several tons of fallen masonry and, to hide one's tracks, they would have to be replaced afterwards. As he brushed the dust from his hair, de Silva wondered what had possessed him to come on this expedition. It would have been excellent experience for Nadar.

'Anything else to show me?' he asked Prathiv and the caretaker. The men looked at each other and shook their heads.

They retraced their steps to the caretaker's room. De Silva's mood improved with the fresher air and he relented and gave both men a tip for their efforts. He noticed that old Prathiv eyed the caretaker's tip sharply. No doubt it wouldn't be long before he suggested another game of dice.

As he strolled up to the Morris, de Silva consoled himself that the afternoon hadn't been entirely wasted. At least he had a slightly better understanding of the theatre now. And in the light of that understanding, it seemed more important than ever to question Kathleen Danforth and her maid.

His thoughts went back to Jane's theory. Was it really

too farfetched that all of the cast had conspired to murder Danforth? It could explain away the difficulties. He frowned. But would there have been time to commit the murder? Possibly. Suppose the caretaker had been involved and lied about the time some people went to the green room? Nadar had already said that the man was known to be a gambler and untrustworthy. Might debts make him malleable? Or perhaps he simply wasn't as vigilant as he professed to be. That was perfectly possible.

A pair of langur monkeys leapt off the bonnet of the Morris and scattered as he approached. He shook his fist then turned anxiously to inspect his beloved car. The wretches were fond of shiny things and the chrome fittings might have tempted them.

He had just satisfied himself that there was no damage when he heard a voice behind him. He turned to see the caretaker. Now what? He doubted he was going to hear a sudden confession of guilt.

The man cast a glance over his shoulder then his eyes returned to de Silva.

'Have you something else to tell me?'

The man hesitated.

'Out with it then.'

'It may be nothing, sahib.'

'I'll be the judge of that.'

The caretaker's eyes slid to de Silva's pocket. He felt a surge of irritation.

'Do you understand that I can arrest you for hiding something that might be important?' he snapped.

The caretaker looked chastened. 'Forgive me, sahib.'

'So, what is this you wanted to tell me?'

'I saw a man outside the theatre one evening. It was before Sahib Danforth was killed.'

De Silva raised an eyebrow. 'I expect you see many men

outside the theatre. Was there anything unusual about this one?'

'I had gone to put something outside the stage door when I saw him in the shadows. He didn't notice me at first. He looked as if he might want to come in, but when I went out to ask what he wanted, he didn't speak and hurried away.'

'Did you see his face?'

The caretaker shook his head. 'Not clearly.'

'Was he short or tall?'

The caretaker indicated a point a few inches above de Silva's head.

'Thin or fat?'

The caretaker held his hands wide apart. 'Big, and a white man, I think, sahib. He was dressed in British clothes. I did not see his face but he was holding something behind his back.'

'Did he come again?'

'No, sahib.'

De Silva sighed. This wasn't getting him anywhere. 'Well, if he does, make sure you get a better look. And then tell me.'

The caretaker looked downcast. 'Yes, sahib.'

De Silva watched him go back into the theatre. He wondered if the tip was already in old Prathiv's pocket. The caretaker would have to do better than some vague story about a loitering man if he was hoping for another one.

He started the engine and put the Morris into gear. He looked forward to getting home and unburdening himself to Jane over a cup of tea in the garden.

CHAPTER 9

'Perhaps you'll be able to catch Archie on his own and have a word with him,' Jane said encouragingly.

The Morris bowled along the leafy lanes that led to the cricket ground; afternoon sun filtered through banana trees and coconut palms, glinting off its smart navy paintwork. De Silva's fingertips beat out an irritable rhythm on the steering wheel.

'I hope so. Danforth was killed on Tuesday and now it's Saturday. Naturally, his widow and his mistress, if that's what Emerald Watson really is, will still be very distressed, but is it reasonable to deny me access to them for so long? I'd like to think that Archie places some faith in my ability to be tactful.'

'I expect he does, dear. But this has come as a shock to everyone.'

'Murder has a way of doing that.'

Jane sighed. 'Don't be tetchy, Shanti. You know what I mean.'

'Sorry.'

She patted his arm. 'I must say, I was quite surprised that the cricket wasn't cancelled, but according to Florence, Kathleen Danforth was most insistent that things shouldn't change on her account. She won't be here, of course, but it's good of her to take that line at a time like this.'

'The famous British stiff upper lip?'

'It is one way of getting through these terrible occurrences, dear. Although I understand that Mrs Danforth is Irish, as her husband was, and they tend not to be as phlegmatic as the English. It must be their Gaelic blood.'

'And have you discovered anything new about Emerald Watson?'

'She's from somewhere in the Home Counties I believe, and she hasn't been on the stage long. Peggy Appleby probably knows more about her. You could try speaking to her. As I think I've told you, she and Emerald have become good friends.'

'I'd far rather speak to the lady herself.'

'Well, let's hope Archie will unbend before too long.'

'It would be a relief.'

The cricket ground was already busy. Play started at eleven, but de Silva had wanted to spend an hour or two in his garden before he and Jane came out. He'd felt in need of some time with his plants. Unlike humans, vegetables and flowers were refreshingly free of idle curiosity. He hoped he wasn't going to have to fend off a lot of questions about the murder and how he was progressing with finding the culprit. By now it was inevitable that it would be a hot topic of conversation around town, and he wasn't much comforted by Jane's assurance that people were far more likely to be talking about the news from England that the King planned to marry his American mistress.

They found a parking place and headed for the pitch, arriving just in time to see Doctor Hebden go in to bat. The teams were both drawn from Nuala's own players and de Silva saw that his sergeant was bowling and Constable Nadar fielding at short leg.

'Ah good,' said Jane, shielding her eyes against the sun. 'There's still room in the covered stand. We won't have to manage without shade. But I brought a parasol, just in case.'

De Silva pointed to a row of big-bellied clouds in the

far distance. 'You might be needing it later. We could have a splosh of rain.'

'A splash, dear. Although splosh is very expressive. It makes me think of children jumping in puddles. You know, when I came to Ceylon, I thought it only rained during the monsoon. It was quite a surprise to find that there was some rain in between.'

'Just as well, or the garden would be harder to care for.'

'Oh look, talking of Peggy Appleby, there she is with her husband. And I do believe that's Miss Watson with them.'

De Silva scrutinised the three people she pointed to – a plump, fair-haired young woman in a fuchsia frock; a tall man in the ubiquitous cream linen suit and panama hat of the British in Ceylon, and another young woman. Yes, it was Emerald Watson.

'Peggy must have persuaded her to come.' Jane frowned. 'Shanti, do you really think that she was Danforth's mistress? I don't want to sound prim and I know these things happen, but I'd be surprised if Peggy knows.'

'Why do you say that?'

'Because I doubt she would be so friendly if she did. The Applebys are a very conventional couple. I think Peggy would be shocked.'

'Then she probably doesn't know and I only have the word of the men in the company for it. They may have their reasons for wanting me to think that Danforth and Miss Watson were having an affair.'

'What would they be?'

'They might want to divert suspicion from themselves by putting it in my mind that Kathleen Danforth had good reason to want her husband punished, maybe using Paul Mayne to help her do so.'

'But you told me you can't see how he would get to Danforth's room unobserved.'

He sucked air through his teeth. 'That's a problem.'

Jane glanced at the tea tent where a bevy of Nuala's ladies dressed in floral finery were busy with large enamelled teapots and hot water urns. 'It looks like tea won't be long. We'd better find a place to sit if we want to see anything beforehand.'

Although he usually enjoyed watching cricket, it didn't hold de Silva's attention that day. He was more interested in observing the Applebys' little party. The husband looked absorbed by the game, but his wife was obviously more concerned with their guest. Peggy Appleby's blonde curls glinted in the sunshine as she talked. Emerald Watson, on the other hand, seemed to have little to say. De Silva wondered whether he should try to engineer a chance meeting in the tea interval but decided against it. In such a public place, it would be impossible to do anything but make small talk, and there was a distinct chance even that would get back to Clutterbuck and arouse his wrath. No point in doing so without a good reason.

When play stopped for tea, he noticed that David Hebden lost no time in joining the Applebys' group as they strolled towards the tea tent.

'Do you see what I see?' Jane whispered as they joined the crowd heading in the same direction. 'Doctor Hebden is definitely taking an interest in Miss Watson's welfare and I'm sure it's not just professional.'

'Well, whatever it is, I'd prefer not to meet them just at the moment.'

'I suppose that's wise. It's hardly the time to ask Emerald Watson anything.'

'Quite.'

Jane shaded her eyes. 'Oh look, there's Florence coming this way with Archie in tow. I'm afraid it's too late if you want to avoid them too.'

'I don't think that's necessary. Perhaps an afternoon of cricket will have put Archie in a mellower mood than last time we spoke. Would you try and steer Florence away and give me a chance to raise the subject of the ladies again?'

'I'll do my best.'

She waved. 'Florence! How nice to see you, and dear little Angel too,' she added, beaming at the furry bundle tucked under Florence's arm. 'He's fully recovered, I hope?' She patted the little dog's head.

'Good afternoon, Jane. He has, thank you.' Florence turned to de Silva. 'We've had such a time of it, Inspector. Angel escaped for a few hours and it took four of the servants and all the gardeners to find him.'

De Silva suppressed a chuckle at the idea of ten grown men pursuing a small, recalcitrant dog. It must have looked like a scene out of the Keystone Cops.

'I'm sorry to hear it, ma'am, but very relieved he was found. I trust he came to no harm.'

'Luckily not, but I've given the servant who let him slip his collar a severe reprimand.'

Possibly the servant had greater need of sympathy than his escaping charge, thought de Silva.

Archie Clutterbuck had stopped to speak to someone but now joined them. He greeted Jane with a smile but de Silva sensed that his own welcome was not quite so warm.

Jane put a hand on Florence's arm. 'I'm so glad we met. If you can spare me a few moments, I've been wanting to talk to you about the church flower rota for the Christmas display.' She lowered her voice conspiratorially. 'I'm not sure that the vicar's wife has arranged enough people for it. I'd speak to her myself but you will do it so much better than I could.'

With concealed amusement, de Silva observed how Florence's nostrils flared like a warhorse's at the bugle call to battle. As Jane drew her away, he took a deep breath.

Archie Clutterbuck raised an eyebrow. 'I don't need a crystal ball to tell me what you're going to ask, de Silva,' he said in a low voice. 'My diary's been crammed full to bursting for the last few days but I'm aware I've been neglecting this Danforth business. Here isn't the place to discuss it though.'

'Of course, but I would like to fix a meeting to do so as soon as possible, sir.'

'Very well,' Clutterbuck said with a sigh. 'You'd better come up to the Residence tomorrow morning. Half past eight. Will that satisfy you?'

De Silva frowned. He found the assistant government agent's attitude increasingly puzzling. It was almost as if this death in their midst was a tiresome distraction from more important matters. Clutterbuck was right though, this wasn't the place to go into detail. A Sunday morning meeting would have to satisfy him.

CHAPTER 10

The morning air was still pleasantly cool as de Silva parked the Morris on the gravel sweep in front of the Residence and climbed out. No gardeners were at work and the only sounds were the liquid calls of birds in the trees. Refreshed by their night-time respite from the heat of the sun, geraniums, marigolds, petunias, and begonias stood to attention in the formal flowerbeds. He would have enjoyed the sight if he hadn't been apprehensive about the reception he was about to receive.

The servant who answered the door let him in and ushered him into the small room off the hall. Anticipating a long wait, de Silva picked up one of the old motoring magazines lying on the table and flicked through, but not many minutes passed before the servant returned to say Clutterbuck was waiting for him in his study.

De Silva stood up, straightening his jacket. 'Thank you.'

In the study, Darcy, Clutterbuck's elderly Labrador, lumbered up from his place by his master's feet and came to greet him. De Silva fondled the dog's ears. At least someone was pleased to see him.

'Good morning, sir.'

'Good morning, Inspector.' Clutterbuck didn't rise from behind his desk. 'Well, you'd better take a chair and fill me in.'

De Silva sat down opposite. The light from the window

behind his boss's head cast it into shadow. In front of him, the desktop displayed the accoutrements of a busy colonial administrator, combined with mementos of Clutterbuck's leisure interests: an ashtray decorated with a picture of a leaping salmon; a small bronze statue of a hunter squinting through the sights of his rifle, and a silver trophy engraved with the words *The Royal Nuala Golf Club Championship 1932*. It was a world away from the life of an actor in a travelling theatre company.

'I understand you interviewed the men at their hotel,' Clutterbuck went on. 'Unfortunate I wasn't able to be present but I'm sure you did a good job without me.'

This was a promising start at least. Perhaps the meeting was going to be less fractious than he had feared.

'Have you come up with any leads?'

'Not yet, I'm afraid.'

'Hmm,' mused Clutterbuck when he explained about the layout of the theatre, the security measures, and the caretaker's claim that he was always at his post, except for the rare occasions when his predecessor took over from him.

'Do you believe the man? Did he seem trustworthy?'

'I would describe him more as *slippery*. My constable knows a little about him and says he is a gambler and very boastful.'

'I see; so, he might be willing to turn a blind eye if someone didn't want it known they had crossed the lobby for a nefarious purpose.'

'It's a possibility, but he may be telling the truth. If so, that leaves only Mrs Danforth, and perhaps her maid, at the same end of the theatre at the time in question. That is why I am most anxious to interview them.'

A thunderous expression darkened Clutterbuck's face.

'Are you accusing the lady of killing her husband, purely because you have some unreliable fellow's word for it that no one else was at that end of the theatre? It's absurd! My wife and I met the Danforths on several occasions and they were clearly a devoted couple. It could be someone outside the company entirely. A thief, say, whom Danforth surprised.'

De Silva had already rejected that idea as implausible but it was always unwise to be dismissive with Archie Clutterbuck. 'You make a good point, sir,' he said politely. 'But then Mr Danforth was a strong man. I doubt he would have given in without a fight and it didn't look as if he had made any effort to defend himself.'

'He may have been asleep. Didn't that man Sheridan say he left him to have his rest?' Clutterbuck looked irritable and de Silva suspected that he shared his own initial reaction that it was impossible to imagine such a beautiful woman as Kathleen Danforth committing such an ugly crime.

'I don't intend to make any assumptions, sir,' he said evenly. 'I never come to my conclusions without firm evidence.' He hesitated for a moment then decided to risk pressing the point. 'But the lack of signs of a struggle leads me to believe that Mr Danforth knew his attacker and trusted them, or he had been drugged. I would be surprised if he was sleeping so deeply that he wasn't roused into putting up some kind of fight. And going back to the men, Sheridan, Morville, and Raikes all claimed Kathleen Danforth and Paul Mayne were having an affair. Mayne was defensive about it, but he admitted there was something between them. Danforth might have been jealous and threatened them, or they wanted him out of the way. That would give them a motive for murder.'

Clutterbuck flushed. 'I'm not interested in gossip, de Silva. Give me facts.'

By the time de Silva finished, Clutterbuck was frowning. 'It strikes me,' he said, 'you should be leaning harder on this caretaker. I maintain that the most likely explanation is the attacker was an intruder who got past him and hid in the theatre. Danforth caught him unawares, he panicked and seized the first weapon that came to hand.'

He stood up, rousing Darcy, who staggered to his feet with a grunt, tail wagging. 'We'll have to wrap this up now. Time for church and I must make an appearance. Keep me informed, won't you?'

'There's one more thing, sir,' said de Silva, trying hard to control his irritation at Clutterbuck's attitude.

'Yes?'

'The caretaker mentioned he'd seen a man loitering near the theatre one evening. He was hiding something behind his back. When the caretaker called out to him, he hurried away without answering.'

'Let's not clutch at straws, de Silva,' snapped Clutterbuck. 'It was probably a beggar afraid he'd get a beating.' He brightened. 'Or it bears out my theory, and it was this thief watching for his chance to get in.'

'Unlikely, sir. The caretaker said the man looked British and was respectably dressed.'

There were footsteps in the corridor and a knock at the door. A servant entered.

'The car is waiting, sahib.'

'Right. Thank you, de Silva, we'll have to leave it for today. I'll make arrangements for you to visit Mrs Danforth and Miss Watson and you'll be notified.' He nodded to the servant. 'You may show the inspector out.'

De Silva felt his cheeks burn as he followed the servant back to the hall. There were times when he found the assistant government agent's attitude infuriating and this was one of them. To his relief, they didn't meet anyone on the way to the front door. It would have been hard to make polite conversation with Florence. Outside, he walked back to the Morris, resisting the urge to kick trenches in the

Residence's immaculate gravel as he went. He hoped the sermon the Reverend Peters had prepared for the morning service was a long and very dull one, then felt remorseful. Jane would be there having to put up with it too.

Driving away, the cool air rushed up into his face like balm, but it did not soothe his wounded pride. That would take several hours of contemplating his garden.

* * *

'How did it go?' asked Jane on her return from church. He'd been home for a couple of hours but was still not feeling much better, in spite of a quiet perambulation round his flowerbeds.

'Archie was in one of his difficult moods.'

Jane unpinned her navy hat and put it on one of the verandah chairs.

'He fastened on the fact that the caretaker may be an unreliable witness and he's got the idea in his head that the murderer has nothing to do with the company,' he went on.

'Does he have any suggestions who it might be then?'

'He favours the idea that it was a thief who broke in and was hiding in Danforth's dressing room.'

Jane's brow puckered. 'But you found Danforth facing his dressing table. Surely he would have seen an attacker reflected in the mirror and tried to save himself?'

'Exactly. And if he was resting as Archie went on to suggest, it's more likely he would have lain down on the bed than dozed off in his chair.' He scratched his chin. 'I'm still waiting to hear whether there's firm evidence that Danforth was drugged before he died. If he was, the theory that it was a random break-in would be even less plausible. It has too many holes in it as it is.'

'But who would have drugged Danforth and when would they have the opportunity?'

'I wish I knew.'

'Shanti, I had a thought while I was at church—'

'Reverend Peters' sermon didn't engross you then?'

'Poor man, his sermons rarely do, but my idea might be worth considering.'

'Go on.'

'Do you remember the uprising in Chittagong?'

De Silva had to think for a moment before it came back to him. A revolutionary group, many of them young, had carried out a plan to take over the Bengali city, and the British were caught unawares. The first target was the Telephone and Telegraph Office. It was destroyed in less than five minutes, the switchboard smashed and the whole place stripped. Immediately after that, a separate band of revolutionaries attacked the Police Lines' armoury. Their military-style uniform confused the guard who was shot dead. Other revolutionaries damaged the railway lines to make it harder for the British to bring up troops. The British club was taken and the wireless station on the only ship in port put out of action.

The next day however, the uprising that had, at first, looked unstoppable turned into a fierce battle when the British began to fight back with weapons from an armoury the rebels had overlooked. Well-trained and equipped troops were brought up too and the rebels were soon crushed.

'Yes, I do,' he said. 'The British over here were very worried the unrest might spread to Ceylon, but we remained peaceful. Why do you bring it up now?'

'Do you remember the date of it, Shanti?'

He pondered a moment. 'It must be about six years ago.'

'Yes, but I meant the exact date. It was on the eighteenth of April and that was significant. The rebels chose it because it was the date of the Irish rising against the British in 1916. The Irish called it the Easter Rising and the rebels in India gave their revolt the same name.'

A deep line etched itself between de Silva's brows. 'But what does that have to do with Alexander Danforth?'

'Don't you see? He was Irish. The southern part of Ireland gained partial independence from the British in 1922, but they still have a British Governor General as Ceylon does and they are ruled by our King. Most of the Catholics down there want the British out completely and they want the north back too.'

De Silva frowned. 'And what does the north want?'

'To stay British. Most people in the north are Protestants.'

He searched his memory for facts about Catholics and Protestants. Ah yes, King Henry VIII. He had broken with the pope in Rome and declared himself supreme head of a Protestant English church so that he could marry Anne Boleyn. There had been battles between Catholics and Protestants ever since, but how was it relevant here?

'I'm afraid I'm still having trouble understanding where Alexander Danforth's murder fits into all this,' he said.

Jane sighed. 'Oh, perhaps I'm seeing shadows where there are none, but I can't help thinking of Mrs MacFarlane, the mother of the children I was governess to in Colombo. Mr MacFarlane was Scottish but she came from Northern Ireland. She often spoke of how saddened she was by the violence between the rival factions in Ireland – people injured, even murdered, and homes and livelihoods destroyed. The troubles still go on today and show no sign of coming to an end. What if Danforth was visiting all the countries he went to with more than just putting on plays in mind? A travelling theatre company would make a good cover. It would provide plenty of opportunities for carrying messages and meeting with disaffected people in different areas.'

De Silva chewed the idea over. He remembered the

unusual interest Danforth had taken in Nuala's affairs. Then there was the lavish spending. The Crown Hotel certainly didn't come cheap, and neither did hiring a Lagonda. From what he had heard, the profits of the theatre company wouldn't be enough to support such a lifestyle, so where had all the money come from? Did Danforth have a secret source of income?

'Are you suggesting that he was a spy working for the Irish against British interests abroad?'

'Do you think it's too farfetched? It's a very difficult time for the country with this business of the King wanting to marry Mrs Simpson. If he won't give her up, everybody says it will bring on a constitutional crisis. The Irish might see us as being particularly vulnerable at such a time.'

De Silva considered her point. Of course, Jane was right about the danger of a constitutional crisis. The alarming news, alarming at least to the British, had only just broken in Ceylon and, in England, it hadn't been public knowledge for much longer. King Edward was officially the head of the Church of England which prohibited marriage if either of the couple were divorced. If he persisted in marrying his twice-divorced mistress, Mrs Simpson, he would almost certainly have to give up his crown.

'So few British monarchs have abdicated, and then not voluntarily,' Jane went on. 'It would shake Britain and the Empire to the foundations.'

'Well... I suppose you're right about it being a tempting time for the Irish to make trouble. And although Ceylon may not be of huge importance to the British, it is very close to India which is far more so.'

'And don't forget there was an attempt on the King's life only a few months ago and the man the police arrested was Irish.'

De Silva recalled the story being broadcast on the radio. The British had been shocked and angry. The would-be assassin, armed with a revolver, had been apprehended by the police on Constitution Hill in London. He had hidden in the crowd assembled to see the King drive back to Buckingham Palace after attending a military ceremony.

'Alright, I'm willing to be persuaded.'

Jane smiled triumphantly. 'There! So perhaps the British government had found Danforth out and wanted to be rid of him.'

'Whew! If you're right, it would explain why Archie is acting so strangely. He really needs this murder to look like a random attack.'

'When in reality, it was a political execution. But what if they were wrong about Danforth and an innocent man died? It's too dreadful to contemplate.'

Silence fell.

'What are you thinking, dear?' Jane asked after a few moments.

'If you have found the answer, I'm thinking about how the murder was carried out.'

'Maybe the man loitering outside the theatre got in when the caretaker's back was turned, or climbed in through that window in Danforth's dressing room. One of the cast could have been helping him.'

'If one of the cast is also an agent for the British, why didn't they just carry out the assassination on their own?'

Jane shrugged. 'Perhaps the British authorities didn't trust them to do it and wanted to make sure someone else was present in case they lost their nerve or bungled it.'

'Do you think their role would primarily have been to drug Danforth in advance so that the stranger could finish the job and make sure he never woke up?'

'I think that's likely.'

A memory stirred in de Silva's mind. Danforth's corpse had smelt faintly of brandy but he didn't recollect finding a bottle or a glass in the dressing room when he searched it that night. He grimaced. Foolish of him to have overlooked that. If Danforth had drunk the brandy in his dressing room, who had taken the bottle and the empty glass away?

'You said that Frank Sheridan and Bert Raikes both seemed extremely loyal, but it might change things if they thought their boss was a traitor,' said Jane.

'It might.'

She frowned. 'What about Michael Morville? He didn't want to talk about what he did in the war, did he? Pen pushing might mean anything from ordering blankets to being in the Secret Service.'

A cloud settled over de Silva's head as he weighed up the odds that Clutterbuck had something to hide. If he has, thought de Silva, I'm standing on the brink of some very murky waters indeed. No doubt Clutterbuck would keep his word and let him speak to Emerald Watson and Kathleen Danforth, but it was a forlorn hope that either of them would divulge anything useful. If Danforth had led a double life, he had probably kept it a secret. On the other hand, if they knew about it, they wouldn't want to incriminate themselves.

Jane put a hand on his arm. 'You look cross.'

'I am. I don't like being kept in the dark, if that's what's happening.'

'You'll find a way round it, I know you will. Now, I think what you need is a good lunch.'

CHAPTER 11

Archie Clutterbuck emerged from an official car as the Morris drove up to the Crown. The sprawling, mock-Tudor hotel was the best in Nuala. The Danforths and Miss Watson had been more luxuriously housed than the rest of the cast. It seemed strange that Kathleen would put up with her husband flaunting a mistress so close to home. De Silva still wasn't sure whether to believe the story of the affair. Was it just a malicious rumour?

Clutterbuck hailed him and they walked in together. The grand lobby, with its sumptuous decoration of carved wood and Art Nouveau stained glass, was quiet, and the receptionists behind the desk, smartly turned out in navy and gold hotel livery, sprang to attention. Clutterbuck strode over to them and de Silva followed, feeling like a tugboat in the wake of an ocean liner. Soon, they were being ushered into a lounge on the first floor where Emerald Watson waited for them.

De Silva had given a lot of thought to how he would conduct this interview. He wanted to find out what Emerald Watson knew about Danforth but he needed to be as tactful as possible. He didn't want her upset as that would be bound to annoy Archie and he was already uncooperative enough.

When he'd first seen her, Emerald Watson had reminded him of one of those bright-eyed, outdoorsy girls who featured in many of the detective novels Jane favoured. Girls who captained their school hockey team and who, on reaching their adult years, played a capable game of croquet or tennis at country house parties where murders seemed to occur alarmingly often. To add a romantic dimension to the plot, they usually stole the hearts of at least one of the young men who were fellow invitees. Today, however, sadness dimmed the sparkle in her eyes. Her face was bare of makeup and she looked very vulnerable.

'It's good of you to see me, ma'am,' he said gently after Clutterbuck had spoken for a few moments. 'This must be a very distressing time.'

'Distressing for all of us, Inspector, but life has to go on. So, how can I help you?'

'I'd be grateful if you'd tell me where you were on the evening that Alexander Danforth died.'

'At the theatre. We all were. There was to be a dress rehearsal for our next play, an eighteenth-century comedy. You may recall, we saw you in town and mentioned we were going to those caves beforehand. We returned to the theatre by three o'clock. Alexander had some business to discuss with Frank Sheridan so I went to my dressing room. I rested for a while then went over some lines. I need to put in more work than the others, you understand. I'm very new to all this and afraid of letting everyone down, although Alexander was always so kind about…'

Her voice cracked. He waited until she had composed herself.

'I changed into my costume at around half past five and went along to the green room. When Alexander was late joining us, Frank went to see if something was wrong.' She broke off and swallowed hard. 'You know the rest,' she whispered.

De Silva saw Archie Clutterbuck shoot him a warning glance. 'We'll put an end to this interview at any time you want, my dear,' he said. De Silva did his best to conceal his irritation.

Emerald gave them both a brave smile. 'No, I shall be alright. I know you need to do everything possible to catch poor Alexander's killer.'

De Silva nodded. 'Thank you for being so understanding, Miss Watson.'

'Would you like me to call for some refreshments, my dear?' asked Clutterbuck. 'Tea perhaps?'

She shook her head. 'You're very kind but there's no need.'

Clutterbuck patted her hand. 'Are you ready to go on?'

She nodded.

'I've been told that your dressing room was one of the ones along the corridor where all the cast members except the Danforths were housed.'

'That's right.'

'While you were in your dressing room that afternoon, did you notice any unusual activity in the corridor?'

'I was asleep for about an hour but otherwise everything was quiet.'

'Then as far as you know, everything was proceeding normally?'

'Yes.'

'Is there anything you can tell me that might help us to find Alexander Danforth's killer?'

He saw that her eyes glistened. She plucked mechanically at a stray thread on the sleeve of her dark dress.

'How long have you known him?' he prompted gently.

She flushed, but there was a flash of anger in her eyes.

'I know what some people think about our relationship, Inspector. Michael Morville and Charles Crichton are civil enough, but Frank Sheridan – well, he's disagreeable to everyone. He never talks to me, but I often catch him staring in the oddest way, as if he wants to eat me.'

She grimaced. 'Bert Raikes is an odious man too. Always finding an opportunity to make snide remarks.'

'Did you mention any of this to Mr Danforth?'

'No,' she said quietly. 'He would have been furious and if he'd spoken out, he would have had to break his promise to Kathleen. I couldn't ask him to do that.'

De Silva was thoroughly puzzled.

Emerald sighed. 'Now that he's gone, I may as well tell you, Inspector. I expect it will come out sooner or later anyway. Alexander and I weren't lovers. He was my father.'

CHAPTER 12

It took a few seconds for it to dawn on de Silva that the news didn't seem to come as a surprise to Archie Clutterbuck. Had the young woman already confided in him? If so, why hadn't he cleared the matter up when the possibility of an affair was first mentioned? Even though he'd seemed dismissive of it, he'd let the suggestion that it might be a contributory motive for Danforth's murder remain on the table. Why on earth hadn't he been more open? It wasn't as if de Silva would have spread the news round Nuala.

'My mother met Alexander before the war and they became lovers. Perhaps she hoped they would marry, but they didn't. When her family found out she was living with him, they were furious and disowned her. Then war broke out. Alexander was posted abroad and it was only after he'd gone that she realised I was on the way.'

'Did she tell your father?'

'No, they'd quarrelled bitterly before he left. She had nowhere else to go, so she went back to her parents. I don't think they made her feel very welcome but they took her in. She was still with them when I was born and she stayed throughout the war. My grandparents were very pleased to have a grandchild and, in wartime, it was so common for husbands and fathers to be absent that it didn't raise any comment. After the war ended, though, and Alexander returned to England, my mother left me with my grand-parents and went back to him.'

Once more, Emerald fiddled with the stray thread on her sleeve. The only sound was the rhythmic swish of the ceiling fan scything the air.

'She didn't tell him about me at that stage,' she went on. 'By then my grandparents felt they were too old to cope with a young child on their own so my mother's sister and her husband looked after me. They lived in a different part of the country to my grandparents so no one needed to know the circumstances in which I came to them. Their name was Watson and that was what they called me. They were childless and they told their friends and acquaintances they had adopted me.'

She paused and closed her eyes for a moment, pressing the fingertips of one hand to her forehead. 'I think I would like that tea now if you don't mind.'

'Of course, my dear.' Clutterbuck went to the telephone and ordered tea. 'Take as much time as you need to compose yourself,' he said when he had sat down again. 'Would you prefer to continue our interview later?'

Emerald shook her head. 'I'm alright. I'm sure the inspector feels he has been patient for long enough.'

De Silva murmured a polite denial.

'Returning to my father was a disaster for my mother. She was already fragile and he found it very hard to cope with. They broke up again but this time, she found no consolation in coming back to her family.' There was a long pause. 'I'm afraid that she took her own life.'

'I'm so sorry, ma'am,' said de Silva. 'What a tragedy for you.'

Emerald smiled sadly. 'My aunt and uncle did their best to shield me at the time, Inspector. It was much later that I learnt what had really happened.'

There was a knock and a servant bearing a silver tray

brought in the tea. When it had been poured out, de Silva raised his cup to his lips gratefully. In spite of the ceiling fan, it was stuffy in the room.

'My uncle and aunt contacted Alexander to tell him the sad news. At last, they told him he had a daughter. It must have come as a shock, but he didn't shy away from his responsibilities. Between them, they agreed that my aunt and uncle would bring me up but he would help out financially when he could. I only saw him a few times and I was still quite young when he took the company abroad, but he stayed in touch all those years.'

Her voice sounded hoarse and she stopped to drink some tea. 'I was told he was my godfather,' she said when she was ready to continue. 'Although I didn't see him, I loved the presents he sent. Dolls in exotic costumes and toys when I was younger, then, as I grew up, lovely dresses made of fabulous silks the like of which I never saw in England. He wrote letters telling me about the countries he and the company visited and the people who lived there. To me, those letters were as magical as fairy tales.

'When I was twenty-one, my father came back to England for my birthday party and told me the truth. He travelled by aeroplane, leaving the rest of the company in Shimla for a few weeks' summer break. I'd never known anyone who travelled by air before. I knew it must cost an enormous amount of money and it seemed so glamorous. Learning Alexander was really my father changed everything for me. At twenty-one, I was free to make my own choices. I decided that I wanted to join the company and travel, and I persuaded him to take me back with him.'

A bold step for a girl who appeared to have led a sheltered life, thought de Silva.

Emerald Watson seemed to read his thoughts. 'Don't misunderstand me, my life in England was very happy, but

I was convinced that a different, more exciting one was waiting for me, and I wanted to seize my chance.'

'Was there nothing you regretted leaving behind?'

'There was a man who was sweet on me, if that's what you mean. He was nice, but I didn't care about him in the same way he cared about me.'

She paused, then a defiant note crept into her voice. 'Friends told me I was mad to send George away. He was well off with a good career. But I know I did the right thing.' She shrugged. 'I suppose my aunt and uncle always thought I would marry and have a family so I wasn't trained for anything much. I can't imagine what I'd have done if I'd stayed in England as a single woman.'

'One thing still puzzles me, Miss Watson. Why didn't you want it known that you were Alexander Danforth's daughter?'

'It wasn't me, or my father, Inspector; it was because of Kathleen. She and my father never had a child of their own and it was a very painful issue for her. Admitting that he had a daughter by someone else, and a grown-up daughter at that, would have been a bitter pill for her to swallow. People just assumed that Father and Kathleen had taken the decision not to be parents. She agreed to my coming out here, but it was on condition that we didn't reveal my parentage without her sanction.'

The admission surprised de Silva. Kathleen Danforth was one of the last people he would have expected to be desperate for a child. How tricky it was to fathom people. She was obviously far more insecure than she gave the impression of being. Then he remembered what Michael Morville had said about her wanting to preserve an illusion of beauty and youth. A grown-up stepdaughter, and a very attractive one too, would not have suited her at all.

'My father didn't want to upset her so he suggested we humour her for a while. He was convinced she'd see reason before too long.'

De Silva glanced at Clutterbuck who was looking strangely uncomfortable. Probably he found talk of complicated emotions and relationships embarrassing.

'But she didn't, and the longer the deception went on, the harder it was going to be to reveal the truth.'

Her eyes brimmed. She retrieved a handkerchief from her purse and blew her nose resolutely. 'I'm sorry I'm so little help to you, Inspector. I want my father's killer punished more than anything, and if I had the faintest idea who was responsible, I wouldn't hesitate to tell you.'

Inwardly, de Silva sighed. Emerald's regret seemed genuine, and, in any case, why would she want her father dead?

Clutterbuck pushed back his chair and lumbered to his feet. 'I think we can bring our meeting to a close now. Agreed, de Silva?'

De Silva stood up too. 'Thank you, Miss Watson, you've been most helpful and, once again, please accept my condolences for your loss.'

'I don't think the inspector will need to trouble you again, my dear,' said Clutterbuck. 'Will you, de Silva.'

De Silva felt mildly annoyed at the assumption, although it was probably correct. 'I doubt it, but all the same I'd be grateful if you would stay on in Nuala for the moment.'

'Of course. As it is, I'm not ready to make any plans yet. David... I mean Doctor Hebden, says there's plenty of time and I mustn't worry about the future.'

'Good advice,' said Archie Clutterbuck with a nod. 'Come along, de Silva. Time we were leaving this young lady in peace.'

He patted Emerald's hand. 'Don't forget to call on me if you need anything.'

She gave him a watery smile. 'You're very kind.'

As they returned to the hotel lobby, Clutterbuck's face didn't betray any emotion. De Silva debated whether to ask him if he'd already known about Emerald's parentage, but decided against it. Whatever the answer, it was unlikely to advance the case and, if Clutterbuck wanted to keep his own counsel, it wasn't the time to challenge him. Better to have Archie on his side, at least until the promised interview with Kathleen Danforth was over.

* * *

As he followed Archie into the sitting room of Kathleen Danforth's suite, de Silva wasn't sure what kind of reception he would receive. Her quarters were certainly luxurious. He'd never seen any of the suites at the Crown before but he imagined that few, if any of them, were as grand as this one. Double doors leading to a balcony stood open. He glimpsed large copper pots filled with ferns and orchids, and two steamer chairs with cream cushions.

A light breeze stirred the long muslin curtains that hung on either side of the doors. The fabric broke on the dark wooden floor like cream over chocolate cake. The furniture would have overpowered any room that was not as spacious as this one, but an effect that might have been forbidding was softened by inviting sofas and chairs, opulently upholstered in golden satin and scattered with embroidered cushions. At one end of the room, there was a massive fireplace. No doubt in such a large room a fire was welcome on Nuala's occasional cold nights, but today the hearth was filled with a magnificent arrangement of cream and yellow roses.

In contrast to all this splendour, the woman who rose from one of the sofas to greet them looked desolate. Now he saw her close to, de Silva noticed that her heavy makeup did not fully conceal the lines at the corners of her eyes and lips. He felt a pang of sympathy for her, then registered her expression in his detective's mind. Would even the most accomplished actress manage to convey such profound sorrow?

Kathleen Danforth extended a slim hand to Archie Clutterbuck; both of his large, blunt ones enveloped it.

'My dear lady,' he murmured. 'Inspector de Silva and I appreciate your courage in seeing us.'

He let her hand go and gestured to de Silva who stepped forward hesitantly.

'I'll try to take up as little of your time as possible, ma'am,' he ventured.

'Oh, you mustn't worry about that, Inspector.' Kathleen Danforth's natural voice had a lilting timbre – a softer version of her late husband's Irish brogue. 'Since my poor Alexander has been taken from me, my time is worth very little. I'm sorry you've been kept waiting for so long. Dear Mr Clutterbuck wanted to protect my privacy, but I knew that couldn't go on. You've spoken with Emerald I expect.'

De Silva nodded.

'Then she's told you she's Alexander's daughter.' Her eyes filled with tears. 'Vanity is a terrible sin, Inspector. Alexander and I argued and I made him promise to keep it a secret but I know he wasn't happy doing so. And now he's dead and it's too late to make amends.'

'There's no evidence it would have made any difference to what's happened,' Clutterbuck said quietly.

She sighed. 'Perhaps not, but I wish we hadn't argued.' A sad smile softened her features. 'Alexander and I often disagreed but trouble between us was soon over. It was hard to be angry with my husband for long.'

De Silva frowned. Had she found it as easy as that to forgive her husband's infidelities?

Kathleen Danforth raised an eyebrow. 'You mustn't believe everything you're told, Inspector. Oh, there were other people for both of us after our marriage, but that never changed our feelings for each other.'

Presumably she included Paul Mayne in that, but her insecurity over Emerald made him wonder if she had always taken such a phlegmatic view of her husband's infidelities. It seemed she was prepared to go as far as besmirching Emerald Watson's character to satisfy her own foibles. It didn't indicate a rational nature. Could a fit of jealousy have driven her to murder? Perhaps, after all, it was wrong to rule her out.

'It would help me if you would tell me exactly what you were doing on the day of your husband's death.'

'I breakfasted here then left for the theatre at about eleven o'clock. When I arrived, my maid, Olive Reilly, was already there. One of my costumes needed altering. I tried it on and she pinned it. When that was done, she had a light lunch brought in for me. It was far too hot to be troubling to come back to the hotel. In any case, I never like to eat much at midday. After Olive left, I went over some of my lines then read and wrote letters. At about five o'clock, Olive helped me into my costume and arranged my hair. As it was a dress rehearsal, she didn't do my face. In this hot weather, I only wear my stage makeup for the public performances.'

'Then you went to the green room?'

'Yes. I believe it was a little before six.'

'Was there a reason why you didn't call for your husband to come with you?'

She gave him a steely look. 'Alexander was never still except when he was preparing to go on stage. Then he liked to be left to himself and I didn't disturb him. He would join us when he was ready.'

'Did you hear any unusual noises coming from the direction of your husband's dressing room that afternoon?'

'None.'

'I'd like to speak with Olive Reilly if she's available.'

Kathleen Danforth turned to Archie Clutterbuck. 'May I trouble you?'

Archie got to his feet with more than usual alacrity. 'Of course, dear lady.'

He went to the telephone that sat on a table by the door and dialled the number for the reception desk. There was a short pause then someone answered.

'This is the assistant government agent speaking,' Clutterbuck said briskly. 'Find out if Miss Reilly is in the hotel. If she is, tell her she's wanted in Mrs Danforth's suite immediately.' He listened for a moment then replaced the receiver. 'They're sending someone to find her.'

He returned to his chair and the three of them sat in silence for a few moments. It was broken only by the rustle of the long curtains draping the doors to the balcony as they billowed gently in the light breeze. Archie Clutterbuck stood up and paced to the fireplace where he remained for a while, apparently examining the brass carriage clock on the mantelshelf. Kathleen Danforth smiled calmly at de Silva, her hands folded in her lap. He thought how becoming her black dress was against her bright hair.

When Olive Reilly came into the room, she seemed familiar, but it took de Silva a moment or two to place where he had seen her before. Near the bazaar: that was it. She was the woman he'd noticed waiting to cross the road. Her bearing was still ramrod straight and now that she was not wearing a hat, he saw that the impression of unbending severity he had received extended to the expression on her face. With her aquiline nose and high cheek bones, some people might have described her as a handsome woman, but he found her chilly air of disapproval too off-putting for that.

Like her mistress, she wore black, but the fabric of her dress looked far less expensive. He noted, however, that it was well cut and showed off her neat waist. He remembered Sheridan saying that she was very skilled with her needle.

'Miss Reilly,' he began when introductions had been

made. 'Mrs Danforth has explained that you were pinning a dress for her on the morning of the day Mr Danforth was murdered. She's told us you arranged for lunch to be brought in, then you went to deal with the alterations to the dress.'

'That's right.'

De Silva reached into the bag containing the scissors that he had brought with him and took them out. 'Do you recognise these?'

He heard Kathleen Danforth's sharp intake of breath and realised he had made a tactless mistake, but there was no helping it now.

The maid's expression remained impassive. 'They're similar to my own, but mine are in my work bag.' She gave him a supercilious look. 'Would you like me to show them to you, Inspector?'

'Thank you, but that won't be necessary.'

'As you please.'

'No doubt your work for Mrs Danforth and the company keeps you busy.'

'I like to be occupied.'

'But I think you found time to visit the bazaar here in Nuala.'

If Olive Reilly was disconcerted, she betrayed no evidence of it, nor did she ask how he knew.

'There's often some little thing I need unexpectedly.'

'And this was such an occasion?'

'Yes, I didn't have the right colour thread to match a costume.'

'Weren't you apprehensive about going alone? The bazaar is a busy place and can be intimidating if you're unused to the way of things here. Wouldn't it have been easier to send a servant or at least take one with you?'

Her thin lips curved in a wintry smile. 'Your concern is very gallant, Inspector, but I'm perfectly capable of looking after myself.'

He was sure she was. That look would freeze most ill-intentioned people in their tracks. He was reminded of the doughty Victorian ladies Jane liked to tell him about who had crossed mountains or penetrated jungles and deserts, armed with little more than a sturdy umbrella and a sharp tongue.

Kathleen Danforth intervened. 'Olive never trusts anyone to do a job properly.' She smiled. 'Even myself. Isn't that right, Olive?'

The blandishment failed to soften the maid's demeanour but her mistress continued to smile, clearly used to her ways. 'If you have no more questions for either of us, Inspector, I'm sure Olive has work to do, and I hope you will forgive me but I am a little tired.'

He had been dismissed, albeit charmingly. Clutterbuck got to his feet. 'In these sad circumstances, you've been very generous with your time, dear lady. I think we have all we need.' He turned brusquely to de Silva. 'Come along, Inspector. Time we were leaving.'

CHAPTER 13

'I was ticked off as if I were that dog of his being shooed off the sofa.'

'I'm sure you're being oversensitive, Shanti. Have another scone and you'll feel better.'

'Perhaps,' he grumbled, putting one on his plate and spreading it savagely with wood apple jam. 'But Archie would do well to remember I have two legs not four.'

'He probably didn't mean to offend you. From what you say, he's a little in awe of this Mrs Danforth. One wouldn't think that anyone could have that effect on him when he's been married to Florence for so long, but Mrs Danforth is very beautiful. Perhaps Archie's the sort of man who finds that discombobulating.'

'Discombobu… what?'

'Confusing.'

He raised an eyebrow. 'English is a never-ending mystery to me. So many words for the same thing. I think you are the one who likes to confuse.'

Jane laughed. 'Let's get back to Mrs Danforth. How did she behave?'

'She was charming, and apparently deeply saddened by her husband's death. I sensed that was genuine.'

Jane frowned as she poured them both another cup of tea. 'But you say Bert Raikes told you that she wasn't exactly a model wife.'

'True, but she insists that none of the men she took up with really mattered to her. More importantly, Emerald Watson came out with a big revelation.'

'Oh?'

'She's Alexander Danforth's daughter.'

'Gracious! That's a surprise. But why take so long to tell people?'

He started to explain what he'd learnt. When he'd finished, Jane nodded. 'I agree Kathleen Danforth's reaction doesn't seem to be that of a rational person, but people often behave in strange ways. She's obviously proud, and her lack of children is a sensitive spot. I expect you're right about her not liking to be reminded she's no longer young too, but one can't help wondering how long Alexander Danforth would have let the situation go on. Sooner or later, he was bound to have realised people were making objectionable assumptions about his daughter.'

'Quite.'

'So, what do we have?'

'Very little,' de Silva said glumly. 'None of my interviews have produced any hard evidence for me to go on, and the speculation about Kathleen Danforth's and Paul Mayne's guilt now rests on very shaky foundations. I'm pretty much back to where I started.'

'It's hard to see why Emerald would want to kill the father she was prepared to leave her old life behind for,' mused Jane.

He reached for the bowl of cream on the table and added a dollop to his scone. 'But I suppose there could be a sinister reason for her coming to Ceylon to be with him. Revenge for her mother's death, or unhappiness in her own childhood perhaps.'

'Somehow I doubt it,' said Jane. 'From what you've told me, she doesn't appear to hold her father responsible for her mother's death, and even though she grew up without her parents, where's the evidence she had an unhappy childhood? According to Peggy Appleby, before the tragedy, she seemed a happy, well-adjusted girl.'

'That's certainly how she appeared to me on the brief occasion that I met her.'

'Do you suppose there's a way of finding out more about the men in the company?'

He rubbed his chin. 'Difficult. There might be some information on record for Raikes and Sheridan when they were in the army, but it was wartime so I don't expect it would be easy to find. Anyway, it was twenty years ago. We're unlikely to turn up anything particularly illuminating. As for the others, I wouldn't know where to begin.'

'How about the maid?'

'Ah yes, Miss Reilly. A ferocious lady who reminds me of Mrs Danvers in that novel *Rebecca* you enjoy.'

'Like Kathleen Danforth, she was already in the correct part of the theatre.'

'That's true.'

He scratched his head. 'But she has no obvious motive, and she's not been with the company for long either. Anyway, how would she leave her room without Kathleen Danforth noticing her do it? Mrs Danforth said she was reading and writing letters.'

Jane sighed. 'How tiresome that we have so little to go on. Perhaps the way to approach the problem is to find out if any of the men could have got to the dressing room from the other side without being spotted.'

'Opportunity being our proof and the motive following on that?'

'Yes.'

'I've been thinking about that. Unless the caretaker's lying and I don't have very good reports of his character so we shouldn't entirely discount that possibility, it seems to me that the murderer's safest route would have been from the cellar where the stage trap machinery is. Once down there, they could have climbed up on stage via the trap and then made off to Danforth's dressing room via the wings. They would have needed to be careful not to make a lot of noise, but I noticed that the stage curtain was closed that night.'

He paused.

'Go on,' said Jane.

'Presumably it was going to be opened at the start of the dress rehearsal so that it was just like the real performance, but of course, they never got that far. Therefore, anyone on stage wouldn't have been visible from the auditorium. The caretaker said one person could operate the stage trap machine even though it would be more dangerous. Now that we think Kathleen Danforth and Paul Mayne are unlikely to be conspirators, we need to work out if someone in the company might have been in league with the murderer rather than actually committing the crime.'

'That's a new angle. Carry on.'

'The cellar route would involve stealing the key to the yard that you have go through to get to the cellar without the caretaker noticing it was gone, or at least removing it for long enough to have a spare one cut in town.'

'Are you saying that the thief was a company member who gave the key to the murderer so he, or she, could reach the cellar?'

'Yes; after that, their job would be done.'

'Are there no ways a member of the cast could have got out of the theatre without the caretaker seeing them?'

'I don't think so. There are front doors, of course, and a side door from the foyer, but how would they get to them from the right hand dressing rooms unobserved? It has to be someone from the outside.'

Jane looked at him thoughtfully. 'Why couldn't it be the front or side door keys that the inside accomplice took?'

'Of course, it might be one of those, but the route would involve more time in the open, so a greater risk of being seen. Unless there's another way that I haven't discovered, I think the most likely scenario is that the murderer was not one of the company, but he was helped by someone who was. That person got them the yard key, and the route was the stage trap.'

'If someone was able to use the trap to get onto the stage, do you think they'd have to leave by the wings to reach the corridor where Danforth's dressing room is?'

'Yes.'

'So why couldn't a member of the company just walk onstage through the wings on the other side and go across? Why must the murderer be from outside, and is the cellar relevant at all?'

'That wouldn't work.'

Jane frowned. 'This all seems very complicated.'

'I agree nothing's straightforward. The theatre's like a rabbit warren.'

'How about drawing a plan? It might help.'

She went over to her writing desk and came back with a pencil and a pad of paper. De Silva smiled. 'No time like the present, eh?'

Jane watched as he began to sketch.

'I won't bother with the front of house,' he said. 'But here's the lobby and the corridors leading off it.'

He drew some more lines. 'This is the stage and these are the wings. The caretaker's booth is here in the lobby.' He paused and pointed with the pencil. 'Do you see? The way the booth is angled means that although someone could slip in or out of the wings near the left-hand corridor without being noticed, it wouldn't be possible on the other side.'

'Yes, I see. What a pity, I thought my idea might help.'

'Unfortunately not. Anyway, I'll get Prasanna or Nadar onto making enquiries about the key. They may as well take the scissors too and see if anyone in town remembers selling them, although I doubt the murderer risked buying them in Nuala.'

He frowned. 'I did see Kathleen Danforth's maid coming away from the bazaar one day, but when I asked her about it, she said she'd been to buy some thread for one of Kathleen Danforth's dresses.'

'Do you believe that?'

He considered a moment. 'I think I do. She's a distinctive-looking woman. If she was up to no good, I suspect she would have adopted some kind of disguise.'

He bit into his scone. 'Mm, delicious.'

'What about Bert Raikes?' Jane asked. 'You told me you noticed grazes on his hands. Could he have got them removing rubble from those passages to the cellar you told me about? Or even climbing down from the window overlooking the yard?'

'I doubt it very much. I'm inclined to believe he was telling the truth when he said he got them from working on scenery. The grazes weren't all that serious and, even if it was feasible, which I doubt very much, moving that rubble would have cut anyone's hands to pieces. As for the window, you'd have to be a human fly to climb down that wall and Bert's not a young man.'

'We're still left with the puzzle of the man who was seen loitering outside the theatre,' said Jane. 'Who knows, it might have been Doctor Hebden hoping for a chance meeting with Miss Watson, but are you going to tackle Archie again? You know, the Irish angle. There has to a reason why someone from outside the company wanted Danforth dead.'

'I'm not sure. I'll have to think about it.' He finished the scone and dabbed his mouth with a napkin. 'By the way, talking of Prasanna, he's been behaving oddly for the last few days. Do you know anything about that?'

Jane frowned. Like de Silva, she had become very fond of Prasanna's wife Kuveni when she lived with them for a short time before her marriage. 'I hope nothing's the matter at home. I'll make an excuse to call and see what I can find out.'

'Good.'

He stood up. 'I'm going to take a stroll round the garden. The gardener was supposed to be mending those holes in the fruit cage and I want to make sure he's done the job properly.'

Jane picked up the small brass bell at her elbow and rang for one of the servants to clear the tea things. 'I think I'll stay here and read for a while. My book's due back to the library tomorrow.'

He peered at the cover which showed a beautiful woman in a very becoming riding habit cantering side-saddle beside a dashing man who wore equally elegant riding clothes and a top hat. 'It doesn't look like your usual fare. Any good?'

'Not bad. It's a Regency romance. I like a change from mysteries occasionally.'

As he crossed the lawn and headed for the kitchen garden, de Silva wished he could have a change from the mystery he had been presented with. It seemed impenetrable.

At least the broken poles on the fruit cage had been replaced satisfactorily and the black netting was neatly fastened back in place. Jane liked to have the summer fruits she had been used to in England, so the raspberries and strawberries were grown to please her. The raspberries were nearly ready for picking, ruby-red droplets loading the spiny green canes. From the rows of low plants in front of them, he smelt the sweet aroma of strawberries warmed by the day's sunshine.

The ruby-red reminded him of the words written on the mirror in Danforth's blood: *the rest is silence.*

Who was so eaten up by the desire for revenge that he

was prepared to kill to get it? Or was that a red herring? Were the British really behind Danforth's death?

CHAPTER 14

Shortly after de Silva arrived at the police station the following morning, the telephone rang in his office. It was Nadar's voice at the other end of the line.

'I have a call for you from Colombo, sir.'

'Put them through.'

He sat back, expecting it to be from the pathology lab about the autopsy. The jovial, booming voice that greeted him was, however, as unexpected as it was welcome: his old acquaintance, Henry Van Bruyn.

'Dr Van Bruyn! It's a pleasure to hear from you.'

'Likewise. I fear it's been far too long since I've managed to get up to the hill country. My wife constantly tells me I should retire, and she's probably right. I'm an old workhorse who ought to have been put out to grass years ago. But my patients seem to think differently.'

De Silva smiled to himself. Even though he was well into his sixties, no doubt Van Bruyn's status as one of the most fashionable medical men in Colombo allowed him to command high enough fees to pacify Mrs Van Bruyn.

'Still, it does a man good to keep busy. Mrs Van Bruyn would probably be complaining within a week that I was under her feet.' The doctor's genial laugh rumbled down the line. 'Now, to the reason I called.'

'I'll be glad to be of assistance if I can.'

'I'm sure, but it's more a matter of the help I may be

able to give you concerning this murder inquiry you have on your hands.'

De Silva's ears pricked up. How did Van Bruyn know about the Danforth case?

'I played a round of golf with the Chief Pathologist on Sunday. He mentioned that this actor fellow Danforth was found murdered in Nuala and his department are doing an autopsy. I'd rather be on the golf course than in the theatre but the name was familiar. I've been operating full tilt for the last couple of days but I got my secretary to check my appointment records. Danforth's wife came to see me a few weeks ago, shortly before she left for Nuala.'

'That's interesting. Are you able to tell me more?'

'Not officially, and I'd be obliged if you'd keep it under your hat, but my golf partner mentioned there was a question of drugs being present in the body. I thought it might be useful for you to know that Kathleen Danforth consulted me about her insomnia shortly after she arrived in Colombo. I prescribed Medinal, or as the Americans call it, Veronal, a barbiturate that I resort to with considerable caution, but she assured me she'd taken it before on the advice of her doctor in England.'

De Silva's mind raced. He had come across the drug before. Used carelessly, or with evil intent, it could result in a fatal overdose. It had a slightly bitter taste and was normally taken in the form of cachets, tiny wafers or capsules made from flour. They had to be wetted before swallowing. It would have been impossible for Danforth to be unaware he was taking one, but suppose someone broke open a capsule and used just a few grains of the powder inside? Would it be undetectable in a strongly flavoured drink? He racked his brains but couldn't remember whether this was one of the drugs that could be detected in an autopsy.

'Even in small amounts, it leaves traces in the body,' Van Bruyn said in answer to the question. 'But identifying which particular barbiturate has been ingested can be more difficult. There are several forms and in many cases, their melting points are very similar.'

'What would be a normal dose?'

'Ten to fifteen grains, depending on body weight – less than a gram. That would be enough to ensure a good night's sleep.'

'And a fatal dose?'

'Between three and a half and four and a half grams, depending on body weight.'

'Would those amounts show up in an autopsy?'

'A high dose certainly. I'm not sure about a minor one.'

'Is it possible that someone might be put into an induced sleep for a short time by being given a small amount?'

'I'm not an expert in toxicology but I believe it might be. You would need a reasonable knowledge of how a patient reacted though. As with a fatal dose, the effect is not instantaneous, sometimes a few hours elapse, and the amount would need to be carefully calculated.'

'Thank you, that's very useful information.'

'Glad to have been of help. I must be getting along now. Patients to see. Give my regards to your wife.'

'And to Mrs Van Bruyn.'

There was a click at the end of the line. De Silva reached for his pen and made a few notes then he sat back in his chair, lost in thought. If Medinal had been administered to Danforth, it wasn't necessarily the case that the person responsible was his wife. But then someone else would have needed to know where to find it. He hadn't seen any capsules or pills in Kathleen Danforth's dressing room. Maybe she had them with her in her suite at the hotel but searching that would be difficult at the moment. Now that he had an idea of what he was looking for, however, it was worth paying another visit to the theatre.

* * *

The dusty parking area was deserted when de Silva drove up, except for a pair of spotted doves foraging for food among the dry leaves that had collected in one corner. He parked the Morris in the only patch of shade and went in. The caretaker looked up warily from a newspaper that lay open at the racing page and rose halfway from his seat.

De Silva nodded to him. 'Don't get up. I've just come to take another look round.'

'Do you need me, sahib?'

'No, you may carry on.'

De Silva's footsteps echoed as he walked down the linoleum-floored corridor. Passing Danforth's dressing room, he thought they would probably have been audible inside. If the actor had been awake, he must have realised that a visitor was on the way. He moved on to Kathleen's room; the same thing applied.

A few days of being closed up with no fans working had made the place unbearably hot. Beads of sweat formed on de Silva's forehead and trickled into his eyes. He mopped them away with his handkerchief and threw the window open as wide as it would go before surveying the room.

He had looked through the makeup on the dressing table before but perhaps he had missed something. He picked up a round green tin decorated with the name *Max Factor* above a picture of a professorial-looking gentleman and prised off the lid. A smell that was both fatty and metallic rose from the parchment-coloured greasepaint inside. More pots and tins contained lighter and darker shades as well as rouge. Another held a black, sulphurous compound that he guessed was kohl. There was a box of face powder and a cut-glass dish in which rested a large swansdown puff. He explored it with his fingertips but only released a dusting of palest pink as fine as icing sugar. He turned the receptacles

134

over one by one, looking for evidence that they might have a false base, but he found none.

The mix of scents and the fine powder that rose into the air made his nose itch. Sniffing, he scrubbed at it with his knuckles before combing the contents of drawers, shelves, and cupboards once more. They yielded nothing. His hopes that he might find a cachet missing a small amount of its powder receded.

With a sigh, he sat down on the dressing table chair and stared absently at his reflection in the mirror. Once more he asked himself who had wanted revenge on Alexander Danforth so badly that they had been prepared to kill him.

When he was ready to start again, he made another search of the room where Olive Reilly had done her work. After everything that had bothered his sensitive nose in Kathleen Danforth's room, he was glad the air was a bit fresher, but again he found nothing. He would have to admit defeat. Either Kathleen Danforth had used up the Medinal that Van Bruyn had prescribed, or she had taken it with her to the Crown Hotel.

A surge of annoyance swept over him, mostly directed at himself. Why had he wasted precious time coming up to the theatre today when he had already searched the place? In his heart, he knew that he was putting off the moment when he had to decide if he was going to tackle Archie Clutterbuck about the British government's hand in Danforth's murder.

Conflicting thoughts warred in his mind on the way back to the station, but by the time he arrived, he was no nearer to a decision. In the public room, he found Nadar alone.

'Sergeant Prasanna still at home, is he?'

'No, sir. He is back but he has gone to the bazaar. One of the stallholders came in complaining that someone has been damaging his goods.'

'Anything of importance?'

'Some packets of food, sir, but the thief left a great deal of mess.'

'I see.' That sounded like it would ease Prasanna back in gently. 'Anything else to report?'

'There was a call from Colombo about the autopsy, sir. They asked if you would ring them back.'

'Get them on the line for me, would you?'

He went into his office and tossed his cap onto the hat stand. This might be the conversation that resolved his dilemma. If some drug other than Medinal was found, or even no drug at all, Kathleen Danforth was a far less likely suspect. Medinal was the obvious drug for her to use as she probably still had some in her possession, so why pick a different one? And if Danforth hadn't been drugged, he was extremely doubtful she, or any woman, would have had the strength to overpower such a big man.

The telephone rang. He lifted the receiver and wished the pathologist good morning. 'Or rather good afternoon,' he added, looking at the clock.

'I hope I'm not delaying your lunch, Inspector?'

'Not at all. I'm eager to hear what you have to tell me.'

In his gravelly voice, the pathologist embarked on a lengthy explanation of his proceedings, finally arriving at the point de Silva was really interested in.

'The barbiturate we found in the stomach, combined with alcohol – and you say the victim had been drinking brandy – would certainly have caused him to sleep. As for how much further matters would have gone, I think it's highly likely he was unconscious but still alive when he was stabbed. Do you know if he was a habitual user?'

'No, but would that make a difference?'

'Undoubtedly. Prolonged use of barbiturates results in the body metabolising them faster, with the result that there's an increase in tolerance. Which means that larger and larger doses would be necessary to achieve the same effect of making a user sleep, and thus the risk of overdose is higher. Alcohol is also a factor in increasing the potency of a dose and, in a drowsy state, patients have been known to take additional doses by mistake. But here, the amount was small. It's my belief that there was no intention to kill the victim by using the drug, merely to sedate him.'

'Was the barbiturate Medinal?'

'It's a widely marketed form, so the assumption is reasonable, but identifying the different types of barbiturate is problematic. The methods available aren't as sophisticated as we would like them to be.'

'Thank you, sir,' said de Silva, politely trying not to sound disappointed. 'I appreciate your help.'

The pathologist laughed. 'Such as it is. Well, I'll be off for my meal now and leave you to yours.'

De Silva wished him goodbye and put down the receiver. Why would someone give Danforth a minute dose and then go to the trouble of stabbing him? Were they simply afraid that a fatal dose wouldn't work swiftly enough and Danforth would be resuscitated? Or was the writing on the mirror in Danforth's blood a grand gesture they had been determined to make? Could it be that the British wanted him to believe there was a connection between Danforth's death and the play, Hamlet, leading him to conclude that the murderer must be one of the actors?

* * *

Jane came out of the house to meet him as he turned off the Morris's engine and put on the handbrake.

'I was listening out for you,' she said smiling. 'I have good news.'

De Silva rolled his eyes. 'I could do with some of that today.'

'Oh dear. Is the case still going badly?'

'I'm afraid so. I went up to the theatre again and completely wasted the morning. When I got back to the station, the pathologist at Colombo telephoned about the autopsy report. He confirms Danforth had taken, or been given, a dose of barbiturate on the day he was murdered, but a small one. He was sedated, but it was the stabbing with the scissors that finished the job.'

Jane held out a hand. 'Come and have lunch. It's gone one o'clock and you must be hungry.'

'I am.'

Seated on the verandah, he told her more about the morning and his conversation with Van Bruyn.

'To sum it up,' he finished, 'I'm fed up with all this shilly-shallying and getting nowhere.'

'You have made some progress, dear. There's the result of the autopsy and Henry Van Bruyn's information.'

'Hmm. In the circumstances, I'm not sure there's enough there to risk arresting Kathleen Danforth. It would mean breaking Henry Van Bruyn's confidence too.'

'You mean Archie won't like it?'

'I'd say that's an understatement, and past experience tells me he's capable of ordering me off the case.'

They sat in silence for a few moments, then he rallied. 'You haven't told me the good news yet.'

Jane beamed. 'Kuveni and Prasanna are going to have a baby.'

'Ah, that's good news indeed.'

'It was Prasanna's mother who guessed. She was rather amused it wasn't an explanation for Kuveni's sickness that they'd thought of, but very relieved, of course. Poor Kuveni's still suffering with morning sickness but hopefully it won't last too much longer.'

De Silva chuckled. 'So, I'll soon have two *family* men on my hands. Parenthood certainly seems to have bucked

Nadar's ideas up. If the effect on Prasanna is the same, it can only be a good thing. Apart from the sleepiness when the baby has given them a bad night,' he added.

'That's better. It's good to see you more cheerful.'

Ruminatively, he chewed a piece of naan bread and swallowed. 'Only on Prasanna and Kuveni's account. I'm still not sure what to do about Archie. What would you advise?'

'Confronting him won't get any easier the longer you wait. I think you should just take the plunge. If he knows it's true that the British are at the bottom of this, he ought to trust you enough by now to give you a hint.'

'And if he doesn't?'

Jane looked serious. 'I'm afraid you may have to back off, Shanti.'

He grimaced.

'I know it would be galling.'

'So if he denies it, do I give up just like that? Where would I go from there?'

'You could have one more try. Speak to Henry Van Bruyn again and warn him you need to pass on the information he gave you. I'm sure he'd understand, and wouldn't he have to disclose it anyway if you made the inquiry in an official capacity? Then tell Archie you need to confront Kathleen with this new evidence. If he's lying to you, if anything will flush him out, perhaps that prospect will.'

A golden oriole landed in the tulip tree nearby and perched on a branch, whistling its fluting song. Ordinarily, de Silva would have enjoyed seeing the bird so close up, but this afternoon, he was too distracted. On a brief acquaintance, he had liked Danforth and, although he would never resort to violence himself, whatever the cause, he felt some pity if the man had lost his life because of his devotion to his principles.

'You're right,' he said with a sigh.

'Is there any news about the key?'

'No, I haven't given Prasanna and Nadar the job yet and it could be a long one.'

Jane looked thoughtful. 'You told me you saw Kathleen Danforth's maid coming away from the bazaar before Danforth was killed.'

'I still doubt she'd take the risk of going undisguised but I suppose I can't rule it out. She's certainly ferocious enough for a stallholder to remember her. I'm hoping any European coming in over the last week or so would stick in their memories.'

'Miss Reilly does sound such a gorgon. Perhaps she will turn out to be the guilty person in the company.'

De Silva shrugged. 'At the moment, I've no idea. I suppose she could be a government agent. A ladies' maid isn't a bad cover. Plenty of opportunity to stay discreetly in the background and keep an eye on what's going on. She has a military background too.'

'If Kathleen was asleep that afternoon, Reilly could have gone to Danforth's dressing room without her noticing.'

'She said she was reading and writing letters, but she didn't mention that she slept.'

'She might feel sleeping in the middle of the day sounds a little elderly,' said Jane.

He laughed. 'Yes, even in our climate.'

'Anyway, she may not have had a choice. Perhaps Reilly knows where she keeps her sleeping tablets.'

'That's true.'

'Or Kathleen Danforth was awake and she and Reilly were in league after all.'

'Stop! My head is spinning!'

'One last idea. From what you've told me, Reilly appears to be a cold woman, but you know what they say, still waters run deep. Maybe she harboured a secret passion for Danforth and killed him in a fit of jealousy.'

'You've been reading romances again, my love.'

'I'm sorry, I'm not being a help.'

'Oh, you are. You've stiffened my resolve to talk to Archie, and this afternoon I'll send Prasanna and Nadar down to the bazaar to see what they can find out about that key. If they come up with something, I ought to get the original from the caretaker. Just because someone asks for a key to be cut in the bazaar, it isn't necessarily the one we're interested in. But I don't want to tip him off without good reason, so that can wait.'

* * *

'Good to have you back,' said de Silva, finding Prasanna had returned to the station. 'And congratulations on your news. Mrs de Silva has just told me.'

Prasanna flushed. 'Thank you, sir. I'm sorry I missed doing my work. I'll make up the time.'

'Good, as it happens I have a job for you straight away. You too, Nadar,' he added as the constable emerged from the back room carrying cups of tea.

'I want you to go to the bazaar and find out if anyone remembers a European man or woman bringing in a key to have a spare one cut.'

'When might it have been, sir?' asked Nadar.

'Any time up until the Tuesday that Alexander Danforth was murdered. Oh, and you may as well take the scissors that Danforth was stabbed with too. See if anyone remembers selling them. If you have any luck in either case, get a description of the customer.'

'We'll get straight onto it.'

'You can drink your tea first,' de Silva said dryly. 'Bring me a cup while you're about it.'

He had turned to go into his office when the telephone

rang. Prasanna picked up the receiver. 'It's a call from the Residence for you, sir,' he said after a moment.

De Silva's brow creased. He hadn't wanted to tackle Archie Clutterbuck quite yet. It would be unfortunate if he'd got wind of something already.

'Inspector de Silva?' It was one of the secretaries on the line. 'I have Mrs Clutterbuck to speak to you.'

The creases in de Silva's brow deepened. Florence's calls were fairly frequent and they usually entailed a command to do something that wasn't entirely within his responsibilities. He wondered what had displeased her this time. Children playing too noisily in the public gardens? Stray donkeys eating the Residence's flowers? He drew a deep breath and prepared his most mollifying tone.

The voice that came on the line, however, was agitated and close to tears. 'Thank goodness I've caught you, Inspector.'

'How can I help, ma'am?'

He heard a sob and the sound of her blowing her nose vigorously. 'My poor little Angel has gone missing again. We've searched everywhere – the house, the gardens, the outbuildings – and there's no sign of him. It's been much longer than last time. I'm terrified someone has stolen him. One of the servants had taken him for his walk and suddenly, he vanished.'

No doubt the servant had wished he too could vanish before he had been obliged to explain the situation to his mistress. De Silva didn't relish the prospect of having to mount a search for a lost dog while he was in the middle of a murder investigation but Florence's distress made her curiously human and it was hard not to feel sorry for her.

'We'll do our best, ma'am,' he said soothingly. 'Try not to worry.'

He heard another stifled sob. 'I know you will, Inspector. I'll stay by the phone. Goodbye.'

With a sigh, de Silva replaced the receiver. 'A change of plan,' he announced. 'We have two jobs to be getting on with.'

CHAPTER 15

By the time they arrived, mid-afternoon torpor had settled over the bazaar. In the area where fresh food was sold,
the crowds of shoppers who came every day to haggle with
stallholders had gone, taking with them most of the pro-
duce that had been laid out early that morning. Only a few
stalls remained open in the hope of late sales, although, to
de Silva's eyes, the leftover fruits and vegetables, and wilt-
ing bundles of coriander and curry leaves didn't look at all
appetising.

The sari and cloth shops were a little busier and custom-
ers still gathered around stalls where huge copper bowls of
spices were laid out for inspection. De Silva's sensitive nose
picked out the fragrances of cinnamon, cardamom, ginger,
and cumin. Shops selling shoes and sandals were doing a
desultory trade; nearby, a vendor presided over a gruesome
array of false teeth arranged on a red cotton cloth.

At the corners of some of the alleys, statues of the Buddha
sat cross-legged, gazing serenely ahead as if looking into
another world. Guttering tealights; half-consumed sticks
of incense; flowers; pieces of fruit, and even small bottles of
lurid-hued drinks had been laid at their feet. Flies buzzed
around, braving the heat of the candles and incense to feed
on the fruit. In the metal-working area, the cacophony of
cutting, hammering and welding had died down, but the
smell of burning kerosene and hot metal lingered.

Delegating the job of finding Angel to Prasanna and Nadar, de Silva started his search among the metal workers and sellers of pots and pans, stalls where one might buy scissors or go to ask for a key to be cut, but he had no luck. Several owners told him that if he came back the next day, more places would be open.

As the sun started to redden in the west and shutters went up on the stalls and shopfronts, he found Prasanna and Nadar.

'I'm afraid we have had no luck either, sir,' Prasanna said. 'There are plenty of dogs around, especially as they like to scavenge at this time of day, but none that fit the description you gave us.'

De Silva felt a twinge of pity for Florence's little pet. The dog was used to living in the lap of luxury. He hoped disaster hadn't befallen it.

'It's getting too late to make more inquiries about the key and the scissors but you'd better carry on looking for the dog until dark. After that, you may go home. Perhaps he'll make his own way back. If not, we'll have to start again in the morning and widen the search area.'

The young men exchanged glum glances. Obviously, searching for a lost dog was not what they had hoped for from police work. De Silva frowned. 'I trust I do not need to remind you that police work is rarely glamorous and often painstaking.'

'No, sir,' they chorused.

He relented a little. 'But I'm sure you've done your best today. Tomorrow I'll join you and we can search together.'

* * *

'We had no luck,' he said, pouring himself a shot of whisky. The soda syphon hissed. 'Goodness knows where the little fellow is.'

146

'Oh dear, poor Florence. She must be so upset. That dog is like a child to her. But perhaps now she'll listen to advice. This isn't the first time he's run away and male dogs do have a tendency to ramble off in search of female company, if you take my meaning. Several of our sewing ladies who have experience of dogs have suggested she'd be wise to have him *done*. She protests that would be cruel but it's really for the best and we have a good vet in Nuala who would do the job well, I'm sure.'

De Silva shuddered. He rather hoped he could avoid being a dog in his next life. Sinking down in his armchair, he took a sip of his drink. 'It was hard not to feel sorry for her. She was almost in tears on the telephone.' He raised an eyebrow. 'But you British. Is anything more important than dogs and tea?'

Jane chuckled. 'I must admit, nothing comes to mind. But seriously, you will search again in the morning, won't you?'

'Of course. And we'll keep trying to find out about the key and the scissors.' He linked his hands behind his head and stretched. 'Is dinner ready soon? I'm hungry.'

Jane glanced at the clock on the mantelpiece. 'About ten minutes.'

He drained his glass and stood up. 'I'll go and wash my hands.'

As he passed the table in the hall, the telephone rang. Automatically, he picked up the receiver. A familiar voice greeted him on the other end of the line.

'De Silva? David Hebden here. Hope I'm not interrupting your meal.'

'No, we haven't eaten yet.'

'Then I'll be brief. I hear the autopsy on Alexander Danforth revealed the presence of barbiturates in his body.'

A glimmer of caution entered de Silva's mind. How did Hebden know that, and why was he interested enough to call?

'De Silva?' The tone of voice was more impatient now.

'May I ask whether your interest is purely professional, sir? If so, I see no problem in making the report available to you when I receive it, but I would be interested to know why you want to see it.'

'Professional? What else would it be?'

What indeed? De Silva smiled to himself. Hebden was a decent chap and, after a few false starts, their professional encounters had been amicable, but it was tempting to twist his tail a little.

'I rather thought you might tell me, sir.'

There was a splutter from the end of the line and de Silva hoped he hadn't overstepped the mark.

'Very well,' the doctor resumed after a brief pause. 'If you must know, I'm concerned about the implications some people might draw from the result.'

'Do you mean that if Alexander Danforth was already unconscious, the murderer would not have needed as much strength and could, consequently, have been female?'

'Exactly.'

'Am I right in thinking you have a difficulty with that?'

'I most certainly do.'

'Doctor Hebden, I'm afraid I cannot change the facts.'

'Ah, so it's true! There were drugs present.' Hebden delivered the words like a cat pouncing on a mouse and de Silva reproached himself. A point to the doctor; still it was too late to retract now.

'I assure you, sir,' he said in what he hoped was a soothing tone, 'I and my men will have no time for gossip and unfounded allegations. Proper procedures will be followed and I will take no steps without good evidence.'

'I'm glad to hear it, Inspector.' Hebden sounded slightly mollified. 'Distressing the ladies must be avoided at all costs. The assistant government agent's views on the matter are as strong as mine. Both Mrs Danforth and Miss Watson have taken the tragedy very hard.' There was a slight hesitation as he cleared his throat. 'I understand the latter lady has confided in you.'

'Yes.'

'So, you know that she must be blameless, quite aside from the fact that it's impossible to credit that such a gentle, defenceless creature would commit such a heinous crime.'

De Silva refrained from remarking that he knew nothing of the sort. He could think of several women in the annals of crime whose feminine charms hadn't stopped them from having murderous inclinations. In fact, from what he'd read of history, the one had often masked the other. But there wasn't a great deal of point arguing with a man as smitten as Doctor Hebden clearly was.

In any case, his instincts told him that Emerald Watson was innocent. She appeared to have nothing to gain from her father's death and, despite the past, her affection for him seemed genuine. He wasn't sure he would have described her as defenceless though. She struck him as being a rather robust young woman who knew her own mind. It was, however, hard to imagine her being less than candid. In the circumstances, he was glad Bert Raikes' malicious remarks about Miss Watson hadn't come to the doctor's ears. On the evidence of his sporting abilities, he probably had a useful right-hook.

* * *

'Who was that, dear?' asked Jane when he returned to the drawing room.

'Doctor Hebden.'

'Oh? What was he calling about?'

'The autopsy report. He'd got wind of the result some-how, and taken it upon himself to defend Miss Watson.'

'Goodness, what did you say?'

'Unfortunately, I let the cat out of the bag before I realised that he was on a… what do you call it? A fishing expedition?'

'Yes, dear.'

'Anyway, once I'd confirmed the rumour, he spoke very hotly on her behalf.'

'They'd be very well suited,' Jane mused when he recounted the rest of the conversation with Hebden over dinner.

'How do you know that?'

'Feminine intuition.'

'Ah, that infallible knack.'

'It didn't serve me too badly when I met a certain police sergeant in Colombo.'

De Silva grinned. 'And there was I in despair, thinking you would forget me in no time.'

She took a sip of water, smiling as she set down the glass. 'It wouldn't have been ladylike to be too encouraging. But I did think you were very heroic the way you chased those thieves who tried to rob me.' She reached over and patted his hand. 'And you looked very dashing in your uniform, even though you were a little out of puff when you came back with the purse they'd dropped.'

He pulled a face. 'That's slanderous! I ran like a leopard.'

'I'm only teasing. I was very impressed. And you were so assiduous about keeping me informed of how the hunt for them was progressing.'

'Purely in the line of duty, of course.'

'Of course.'

'Shall we have coffee on the verandah?'

'That would be nice. I don't feel like reading this evening.'

'Poor dear, you've got too much on your mind, but I'm sure it will all come together in the end.'

'I hope you're right,' he said with a sigh. 'I feel there's still a long way to go.'

He pushed back his chair as she rang the bell for a servant to clear the dishes.

'Perhaps a breakthrough is closer than you think.'

'Thank you for your optimism, my love.'

* * *

The cloudless night sky had sucked up the heat of the day, making it pleasantly cool in the garden. Gazing up at the glittering map of stars, de Silva wished he felt the peace their mysterious beauty usually instilled in him, but it eluded him. Mentally, he went over the dramatis personae in the real-life mystery that faced him. The grieving widow and daughter – or were they? The old friends, Bert Raikes and Frank Sheridan. The young, would-be rival, Paul Mayne. Michael Morville and Charles Crichton, who seemed the most detached members of the company, and Olive Reilly, who was indubitably the most forbidding.

'Drink your coffee and try not to brood, dear,' said Jane. 'It's a shame to spoil such a lovely evening.'

'You're right.' He brought his coffee cup to his lips and inhaled the fruity, caramel fragrance. 'This is excellent coffee too.'

'I'm glad you approve.'

She gave a start as a large flying creature blundered against the glass shade of the outside lamp then flew off in a wide arc to land on the wooden corner post nearby. De Silva observed it with interest. An Atlas moth, the biggest moth in Ceylon, perhaps in the world, and broader than the span of a man's hand. The moth settled, fanning wings whose shades of russet, ochre, buff, and dusty pink looked as if they had been laid on by the most skilful of painters. The contrast with the splashes of white, shaped like arrowheads, on each wing heightened the diaphanous effect.

'What a beauty,' said Jane, recovering. 'So sad they have no mouths to eat with and live only a few days.'

De Silva shrugged. 'That's nature.' He chuckled. 'I hope I am not destined to be one in my next life though; I like my food too much. But if that *is* what's in store for me,' he added ruefully, 'at least it ought to be an uncomplicated life.'

'Why don't we have some music? That might take your mind off the case and we haven't listened to the gramophone for weeks.'

'Good idea. What would you like?'

'You choose.'

In the bungalow, he went to the gramophone he'd bought for Jane on their last anniversary and studied their record collection. Something classical would be soothing. He found a recording of pieces by Debussy and put it on the turntable.

As he settled back in his chair on the verandah, the silvery chords of *Clair de Lune* drifted through the warm night air. Slowly, his buzzing brain calmed. As usual, Jane was right. It was a shame to spoil such a beautiful evening.

CHAPTER 16

Arriving at the station the following morning, he parked the Morris in the shade and went in. In the front office, a Tamil was talking vociferously to Prasanna and Nadar.

'What's going on here?' asked de Silva, using his sternest tone of voice. Quelled, the Tamil quietened down.

'Something about finding the dog, sir,' said Prasanna.

De Silva raised a hand. 'Let him tell me in his own words.' He turned to the Tamil. 'But slowly this time.'

'The animal is close to my house, sahib. I can take you there right now.' A crafty look came over his face. 'I think the English memsahib will be very happy and want to reward me for finding it.'

'That will depend on many things. For a start, how do you know it's the right dog?'

'There have been men coming with pictures to the bazaar.'

Ah, Florence must have sent some of the Residence's servants out with posters. He wondered if a reward had already been mentioned. If so, and this man was telling the truth, it seemed strange he hadn't taken Angel straight to the Residence.

'Well, you'd better show me what you've found. Prasanna, you can come along with us. Nadar, you stay and keep an eye on things here.'

The Morris nosed its way through the town, and,

following the Tamil's shouted directions from the dickey seat, de Silva took a road that led out in the direction of one of the nearer villages. He had to drive very cautiously as the way became increasingly narrow and rutted. Plantations of rubber and banana trees made a dense wall on either side. Soon, he was heartily wishing that the Tamil had managed the business without police assistance. If he hoped for a reward, de Silva was mystified why he hadn't.

When the jungle thinned out, however, and they reached a collection of huts set in a clearing, the reason became clear. A large, lean-to shed with an open front stood at the far end of the clearing. Close by was a muddy pool with a churned-up margin. A little way inside the shed was a fully grown she-elephant, chained by one leg to the wall. A noisy gaggle of villagers crowded around her, retreating quickly when she whacked the air with her trunk or shuffled menacingly towards them on her huge leathery legs. As he got out of the Morris and came closer, de Silva saw the baleful gleam in her small red eyes and smelt the stench of an animal agitated by the proximity of so many excited people.

Half-hidden by its mother's great bulk, a baby elephant peered out at the scene, occasionally adding its juvenile squeak to her angry trumpeting. De Silva's stomach hollowed and his legs turned from flesh and bone to blancmange. He already had a pretty good idea of who else was in the lean-to: Angel.

The animated black and white household mop who was so precious to Florence Clutterbuck looked considerably less animated than usual. In fact, the little dog was curled up asleep on a pile of dirty straw in one corner of the shed. De Silva marvelled that he had got so far inside in the first place, and then that he hadn't already been trampled. The question was, how to get him out again in one piece?

'Where's the owner of the elephant?'

With a great deal of pointing and gesticulating, everyone spoke at once. The she-elephant added her voice, shivering the air into a million splinters. Angel woke up and began to yap.

De Silva turned on his heel and went back to the Morris. It took several blasts of the horn to reduce the cacophony to a mutinous grumble.

He looked at the Tamil who had brought them there. 'Well? Are you the owner?'

A new man separated himself from the crowd.

'Who are you?' snapped de Silva.

'The headman, sahib. The beast is mine.'

This gave rise to a rumble of disagreement. Possibly several of the better-off villagers had an interest in the elephant. They were extremely valuable creatures, capable of prodigious amounts of heavy work as well as earning money for their owners from tourists wanting the exotic experience of an elephant ride.

'Did you send this man to me?' De Silva asked.

The headman scowled. 'No.'

Ah, so by being first with the news, the Tamil had hoped to secure any reward going. He wouldn't be popular now, but that was his problem. De Silva's problem was to find a way of removing Florence's beloved pet from danger.

He edged forward and studied the situation carefully. The shed was about ten yards deep but only half as wide, leaving very little room between the she-elephant and the wooden walls. De Silva glanced at Prasanna's tall, lanky frame but then thought better of suggesting he go in. After all, he was a newly married man. But there was even less room for a middle-aged detective who was fond of his food.

He looked round the villagers who seemed less than enthusiastic about meeting his eye. Well, if no one wanted to go in to rescue Angel, the little fellow would have to be persuaded to come out.

Just at that moment, Angel got to his feet and shook himself. De Silva smiled. Thank goodness the dog was so small, the she-elephant might not even notice him coming out of the shed. But the relief was short-lived. With an insouciant air, Angel circled twice then flopped down on the straw, tucked his nose under his back foot and went to sleep again.

'What shall we do, sir?' asked Prasanna anxiously.

A goat bleated nearby and a lightbulb went on in de Silva's head. He handed his sergeant a few rupees. 'Go into the huts and see if any of the women has a piece of goat's cheese we can buy.'

Prasanna looked a little mystified but he went off, returning after a few minutes with a small, extremely aromatic, white lump wrapped in a scrap of banana leaf. De Silva's sensitive nose wrinkled as he took it and peeled the leaf back. 'Excellent. If this doesn't do the job, nothing will.'

Still alarmed by the commotion she had endured, the she-elephant threw up her head and lashed out with her trunk as de Silva approached. Her short, but sharp, tusks gleamed against the black cavern of her mouth. He waited for her irritation to subside then hunkered down and called Angel's name softly. The shih tzu stirred and looked up.

'Angel! Look what I've got for you, Angel!'

Angel snuffed the air. A sliver of pink tongue emerged.

De Silva waved the cheese about encouragingly. He hoped Angel wasn't such a finicky eater as to refuse anything but the cheesy treats made in the Residence's kitchens.

The she-elephant took a lumbering step backwards. Angel's head jerked round and he let off a volley of yaps. Stars danced before de Silva's eyes and the sweat that had been collecting under the collar of his shirt trickled down his back. His heart thumped; he wafted the cheese again.

'Angel!'

This time the little dog got up and took a few steps out

of the corner. Passing the baby elephant, he stopped and stretched. Collectively, the onlookers held their breath. De Silva backed away a little and then a little more. To be safe, he must encourage Angel to come right out of the shed.

At last, a shout went up as the little dog trotted to de Silva and sat at his feet, paw raised and tail wagging. De Silva bent down and, taking the precaution of grabbing him by the collar, presented the cheese.

'Do you think there will be a reward, sir?' asked Prasanna as the Morris returned to the main road and bowled along in the direction of the Residence, Angel happily curled up on Prasanna's lap.

'Oh, I expect Mrs Clutterbuck's relief will make her generous, but we must see to it that it's fairly distributed. It might be best to give it in the form of food or clothing rather than just money to the headman. You and Kuveni know the sort of trouble that can cause, eh?'

Prasanna nodded.

'She's feeling better, I hope?'

'A little, thank you, sir, although she is still sick in the mornings.'

'When's the baby due?'

'In June, sir. We expect it to be under the sign of Mithuna. My mother is planning the visits to the astrologer for the birth chart. She is already telling all her friends that the child will be extremely intelligent and talented.'

'That's very fortunate.'

Prasanna grinned. 'I know what you are thinking, sir. That all grandmothers say this.'

'And I'm sure this time it will be correct.'

The Morris turned into the Residence's drive and, at the crunch of gravel, Angel stood up, wagging his tail. 'He knows he's home,' remarked de Silva. He reached out a hand and scratched the little dog behind the ears. 'And don't you make any more breaks for freedom, young man. You might not be so lucky another time.'

* * *

'There was a moment when I was seriously alarmed that she would kiss me,' he said as he and Jane sat down to a late lunch.

She giggled. 'I wish I had been there to see your face.'

'Even Darcy seemed pleased to see his little companion back, but Archie was not there.'

'What a pity. It would have been the perfect time to tackle him about whether the British were involved in Mr Danforth's murder.'

'Exactly, but never mind. I will have to hope that I am still in favour when the opportunity does arise.'

He spooned a mound of fluffy rice onto his plate then helped himself to jackfruit curry, savouring the appetising aromas of onions, garlic, and spices. 'This smells delicious.'

'Good.'

Jane forked up a mouthful of the milder dahl curry that their cook had prepared for her. She doubted she would ever like her food as fiery as her husband's.

'What are you doing this afternoon?' he asked.

'There's a committee meeting at the vicarage to discuss fundraising ideas for the new church bell. Florence will be there – if she can tear herself away from Angel that is – and I intend to bask in the glory of being related to Nuala's greatest hero.'

He grinned. 'Quite right.'

A sigh escaped him. 'I suppose I'd better drop in at the station and see if there's anything needing my attention. After that, I'll go and find Prasanna. When we left the Residence, I sent him to the bazaar to carry on looking for someone who remembers cutting this key.'

* * *

Nadar stood up when de Silva arrived at the police station. 'Good afternoon, sir. I hope you had success.'

'I'm glad to say we did. The dog is restored to Mrs Clutterbuck. Anything to report here?'

'Nothing important, sir.'

'Ah well, make me a cup of tea, please. After that I'll get off and see if Prasanna has had any luck.'

Half an hour later, he arrived at the bazaar and started to look for Prasanna. It wasn't usually difficult to spot his young sergeant; he was half a head taller than most of the locals. He had been walking for ten minutes, however, when someone else caught his attention.

Walking towards him was Charles Crichton. It was impossible not to meet and Crichton stopped and nodded awkwardly. 'Good afternoon, Inspector. I thought I'd have a change of scene and visit the bazaar I've heard so much about. Hotel rooms don't take long to lose their appeal.'

'I'm sure they don't.'

'May I ask if there's any progress with your investigations?'

'I'm afraid that's confidential, sir.'

Beads of perspiration glistened on Crichton's brow. He took out a handkerchief and mopped them away. 'I'll be glad when I can move on. I don't suppose you can tell me how much longer you intend to keep us here.'

'Regrettably, I can't, sir.'

'It's not easy for me, you know. I'm not really "one of the gang". Never have been, although Alexander was always good to me. But with him gone…'

The corners of Crichton's mouth sagged, in fact the whole of his fleshy face made de Silva think of a melting pink jelly, the features were so blurred by fat. If he felt like an outsider in the company, it might be worth probing for anything new he could divulge, albeit it would need to be treated with circumspection.

'I'm sorry to hear that. Times like these have a tendency to bring out the worst in people.'

Crichton shrugged. 'Oh, on his own, Morville's a decent enough fellow, and I keep out of the way of Mayne and Raikes, but Sheridan…' Crichton came closer and de Silva smelt sweat and cheap cologne. 'He's always been an awkward customer but now he's going completely off the rails. I should look into him if I were you.' He tapped the side of his nose with a podgy finger. 'A few gaps in his life it might be interesting to fill in.'

De Silva maintained an imperturbable expression. 'Thank you for the advice, sir. I'll bear it in mind.'

'Do that. Well, I won't detain you.'

Watching him walk away, de Silva wondered whether to take this seriously. It might be worth another visit to Sheridan. It would be interesting to know if he was as secretive about his past as Crichton claimed.

As he resumed his search for Prasanna, he passed a stallholder who pressed his hands together and bowed, a cheerful grin on his face. 'Welcome, sahib!' He gestured to the sweetmeats on his stall. 'Please accept something. It is all very delicious.'

For a moment, de Silva didn't recognise the man then he remembered he had helped him a few months ago when his stall had been damaged by a rival. He inhaled the aromas of cardamom, cloves, and honey. 'That's very kind of you,' he said, studying the wares on offer before choosing a deep-fried confection shaped like a rosette. He bit into it appreciatively; it was crisp and still warm from the bubbling pan of oil it had been cooked in.

'Very good,' he said between mouthfuls. 'Thank you, again. No more trouble here, I hope?'

'None, thanks to you, sahib.'

The man grinned again showing stumps of betel-stained teeth. He jerked a thumb at the direction Crichton had gone in. 'The fat Englishman is fond of kokis too, but today he does not buy from me.'

De Silva frowned. 'You've seen him here before?'

'Yes.'

That was interesting. Why had Crichton been at pains to make out this was his first visit to the bazaar?

'Another koki, sahib? Or something else? I have many good things.'

It was tempting but de Silva shook his head. The waistband of his trousers was already snug enough. 'Have you noticed where else he goes?'

'That way,' the man said and pointed. It was the area where, among other things, you found most of the metalworkers.

Interesting.

* * *

The sun was going down in a lake of fire as he drove home to Sunnybank. By the time he arrived, darkness had fallen with the suddenness of the tropics.

Jane was in the drawing room, a book in her lap. 'Hello, dear, how did you get on this afternoon? Any news?'

He shook his head. 'Prasanna and I have scoured the bazaar but no one remembers anything helpful.'

Jane sighed. 'How frustrating for you.'

'It is. But a new lead has come up. Maybe I have been barking up the wrong tree all along.'

'Charles Crichton,' Jane said pensively when he had described their meeting in the bazaar. 'Do you really think the fact he seemed to be lying about it being his first visit there is so important?'

'Not on its own, but added to the fact he seemed very keen to throw suspicion on Frank Sheridan, there may be something worth investigating.'

'Or his warning might simply be genuine.'

Going to the sideboard, he picked up a decanter. 'Sherry?'

'Thank you, just a small one.'

He smelt the rich, fruity tang of amontillado as he poured out a glass and carried it over to her.

'That's possible,' he said, going back to make himself a whisky and soda. 'But of all people, Sheridan and Raikes seem the least likely to want Danforth dead.'

'Why would Crichton be any different?'

'That's what I don't know. I'd like to find out more about him. Tomorrow, I'll go up to the hotel where the cast are staying and see who's around. Morville might be the best person to talk to. If Sheridan is guilty, anything he says is likely to be untrustworthy and, anyway, I don't want to tip him off. He and Raikes go back a long way so I'd have to approach him cautiously too.'

'From what you say about Charles Crichton, he wouldn't be agile enough to negotiate any tight corners to get to Alexander Danforth's dressing room.'

'Definitely not, but I still haven't ruled out the possibility that the caretaker isn't telling the truth. Or Crichton's job could have been obtaining the key.'

There was a knock at the door and a servant came in. 'Dinner will be ready in fifteen minutes, memsahib.'

Jane nodded. 'Thank you.'

As the door closed, de Silva drained his whisky and stood up. 'I'll go and get out of my uniform. As usual, it was dusty in the bazaar.'

'Leave it out and I'll tell one of the servants to launder it and put you out a clean one for tomorrow.'

After dinner, he went into the garden for his evening stroll, enjoying the freshness after the heat of the day. The air was alive with the rustle of nocturnal creatures and the squeak of bats hunting for food. Clouds drifted across the moon, partially hiding the stars. He smelt rain on the air. A shower would be welcome.

At the bottom of the garden, he paused to gaze down at the lights glimmering in the town. Off to one side, where the Residence stood, they burned brighter. He wished he knew what was going on in Archie Clutterbuck's mind tonight. If he could arrange a meeting with him tomorrow, by nightfall he might know the truth, but would it bring an end to the investigation?

Turning a few degrees to the west, he picked out the lights of the Crown Hotel, queening it over the small huddle of other establishments where Europeans liked to stay. The one where Crichton and the others lodged was among them. He wished he could see into their minds too.

Unconsciously, he snapped off a fading flower head from the frangipani tree that leant over the hedge. Peeling the petals away one by one, he ran over the facts of the case. Where were the gaps in his investigation? An image of the theatre rose in his mind, the sumptuousness that the public saw contrasting with the dank, gloomy cellar and the bare yard.

The problematic key still bothered him but, gradually, he began to wonder if he was on the wrong track. What about the window overlooking the yard? Possibly it had been a mistake to dismiss it. If the murderer was agile enough to use it to reach the yard, they would have no need for a spare key. There were no footholds one could see, but a rope would do the job.

He remembered the beam across the stage and the system of ropes, pulleys and weights for lifting and lowering scenery. The place the British called the flies. Would anyone notice if one of the ropes was removed and later put back? It was another task for the morning. He hoped Prasanna or Nadar had a head for heights.

As he turned to go back to the bungalow, something drifted into his hair. He brushed it off and smelt again the sweet, intense fragrance of frangipani. The flower's pale yellow gleamed against the dark lawn. He remembered his mother saying that if a frangipani flower fell on your head, you would have good luck. He hoped she was right.

CHAPTER 17

There was no sign of Prasanna when de Silva arrived at the station the following morning but Nadar was typing at his desk in the public room. He scraped back his chair and stood up. 'Good morning, sir.'

'I hope it will be. Are you on your own? Where's Prasanna got to?'

'I am, sir. He has been here but went straight out to look in some more places in town. He had some ideas in the night about where he might go to find out about the key.'

'Ah, right. Then you'll have to be my assistant. Have you a head for heights?'

Nadar looked surprised. 'I'm not sure, sir. I climbed to the top of the helter-skelter when the circus came to Nuala last year. Will that be high enough?'

'It should be. Lock up, please, and then we'll be off.'

It was strange to think that, less than two weeks ago, he and Jane had arrived at the theatre in such different circumstances. Alexander Danforth had been very much alive then, full of vitality and giving a mesmerising performance as Shakespeare's tragic hero.

Danforth's body was still at the morgue in Colombo, but there was no reason why his funeral needed to be delayed any longer. It would be interesting to see if Clutterbuck stepped in and offered to arrange it. If all his consideration for Kathleen Danforth and Emerald Watson was just a smokescreen behind which the British were hiding, would it extend that far?

Nadar looked admiringly at the theatre façade as they drove up.

'Have you ever been inside?' asked de Silva.

'No, sir, but my wife and I go to the pictures sometimes if my mother or hers will look after the baby. My wife likes the Indian films with much singing and dancing and happy endings.'

De Silva smiled. Once, he had taken Jane to an Indian film and she too had enjoyed its exuberance. The happy ending, however, had been a little too contrived for her practical nature.

One of the main doors to the foyer looked to be open, so de Silva decided to give his constable a more exciting introduction to the theatre than an entrance through the stage door offered.

He drew to a halt in the front parking area then got out and strode up the steps with Nadar following. Inside, two women in shabby blue work dresses with their hair tied up in scarves were busy polishing the brass balustrades of the staircases that led to the Grand Circle. The air smelt strongly of Brasso and cheap tobacco. Lounging by the foyer bar was the caretaker, smoking a roll-up cigarette and making the women laugh with a story he was telling. He stopped abruptly when he saw de Silva and Nadar.

'Inspector!' The caretaker stood to attention and tried, somewhat unsuccessfully, to hide his cigarette. 'I only came to see if the cleaning is being done properly.'

The older of the two women sat back on her haunches and shook out the cloth she had been using. She shot the caretaker an acerbic look then refolded her cloth and resumed her vigorous rubbing. A stifled snort of laughter came from the younger woman.

'Well, since you're here, you can save us a walk and take us backstage through the auditorium.'

'Yes, sahib,' said the caretaker, hastily stubbing out his cigarette in an ashtray on the bar and heading for one of the entrance doors.

As de Silva went to follow him, he glanced over the bar counter, noticing the crates of bottles piled up behind it. Behind them, the space receded into shadow. 'What's down there?' he asked, more out of habit than anything else.

'Only the place where glasses are cleaned and alcohol is kept, sahib, and the side door I told you of.'

'I see.'

Nadar's eyes widened as the caretaker unlocked a door and led them into the auditorium. Hushed and shadowy, to de Silva it didn't look as splendid as it had done on the evening of Danforth's last performance but it was still impressive. The rows of empty, red-plush seats rolled out of the shadows like crimson waves. The cream and gold of balconies and walls brightened the gloom. De Silva smiled to see how tentatively Nadar walked down the carpeted aisle. He thought of Prasanna's reaction the first time he had seen the magnificent lobby at the Crown Hotel.

Through the wings, they were back in the shabby reality behind the theatrical glamour.

'What do you wish to see, sahib?' asked the caretaker.

'The window that overlooks the courtyard you showed me, where is it inside the building?'

'I think it is in one of the storerooms but I am not sure which one, sahib.'

'Take me up there first, then I want to go above the stage.'

The caretaker led them up several flights of stairs to a shabby landing with two doors painted a shade of green that closely resembled the colour used in railway stations and government buildings. Some British factory must have produced rivers of it over the years.

The hinges on the first door protested as the caretaker

opened it. De Silva peered into a windowless room, empty, apart from a broken standard lamp with a torn, ruched pink shade; a dilapidated, chintzy armchair oozing horsehair stuffing, and a vase of washed-out dried flowers. Presumably they were props that had outlived their useful life.

The second room did have a window. De Silva went over to it and looked down into the yard. It was a long drop, but the window was big enough for a slim man to climb out. The gauzy cobwebs clinging to the dirty glass gave the impression that it hadn't been open for some time, but then he noticed the spider scuttling into a crevice between the window frame and the wall. An industrious arachnoid only needed a day or two to weave such a web.

A more interesting question was how a rope would have been secured. The only piece of furniture heavy enough to hold a man's weight was the table standing against the opposite wall. He studied the floor for signs it had been dragged across to the window and found none but it was hard to tell as the floor was reasonably clean.

'Good, we'll move on. I'd like to see if there's evidence that any of the ropes in the flies have been tampered with recently.'

Up in the flies, he marshalled his courage and forced himself to take a cautious step onto the rotting walkway. His stomach churned; the stage was far below, at the wrong end of a telescope. He stepped back quickly.

'Shall I go, sir?' asked Nadar. With a lack of perturbation that de Silva envied, the young constable didn't wait for an answer and set off along the walkway, squatting down when he reached the first group of ropes. Apparently oblivious to the drop only inches from his splayed knees, he studied the ropes carefully, feeling along the coarse hemp, then running his hand along the wood underneath. Even though he was on solid ground, de Silva's guts heaved.

'Well?' he called brusquely. 'Any sign they've been meddled with?'

Nadar stood up. 'Some of the fibres are frayed, sir. It might be wear and tear but it could be that someone has taken a sharp implement to loosen the knots. There's not much dust under here either.'

De Silva felt a tightening in his chest as Nadar bent down and pulled a rope up a little way. 'It's heavy, sir. Someone would need to be strong to carry it. Shall I check the others?'

De Silva inhaled sharply. 'No, that's enough now. You can come back in.'

'There is another possibility though, sir.' Remaining where he was, Nadar pulled out his handkerchief and picked something up in it. As he returned to safe ground, the muzzy feeling in de Silva's head receded and he looked to see what his constable had found.

'Mouse droppings, sir. Their teeth are sharp enough to gnaw at the ropes.'

De Silva sighed. It was certainly plausible.

They followed the caretaker down the stairs and back to the foyer. The man hovered as if he was expecting a tip, but de Silva ignored the hint and dismissed him.

'Did you find what you were hoping for, sir?' asked Nadar as they left the theatre.

'Not really.'

Nadar looked downcast.

'It's not your fault, Constable,' de Silva added hastily. 'Police work needs patience and good powers of observation and on that score, you did a very good job.'

Nadar beamed. 'Thank you, sir.'

A gardener came round the corner weighed down on one side by a watering can and proceeded to water the large terracotta pots of geraniums at the top of the theatre steps. Droplets of water gleamed like silver on the velvety leaves and scarlet petals.

De Silva watched the operation for a few moments then

beckoned. With a clunk, the man dumped his can on the ground and came over. 'Yes, sahib?'

'Have you seen anyone coming or going here over the last few days?'

'It is hard to remember who comes and who goes, sahib. I am on my own and there is much work to do. For little pay,' the man added glumly.

From the evidence of the scrubby land at the back and these few pots, the pay might be poor but the work was hardly arduous. All the same, it was worth a small outlay to get some information.

'Try and remember,' said de Silva, chinking the loose change in his trouser pocket.

The man's eyes glinted. 'When I was sweeping at the back, one of the Englishmen came.'

'When was this?'

'Two days ago.' He scratched his head. 'Maybe three.'

A pity he couldn't be more specific but it might not be important. 'What did he look like?'

The gardener touched the thick hair on his head and grinned. 'An egg, and his body thin like my mother-in-law's dahl.'

It sounded like Michael Morville.

'Did he say anything to you?'

The man shook his head.

'And how long was he here?'

The gardener shrugged and de Silva realised he had no watch. 'Was the caretaker on duty?'

A grin cracked the man's weathered face. 'It was after lunch and he likes a nip of arrack.'

'Ah.'

De Silva handed over a few coins. 'If you see or remember anything else, come to the police station and there may be more. You can get back to your work now.'

Leaving the gardener to his watering, de Silva led the

way to the Morris. A useful encounter. The picture was becoming a little clearer. Now he wanted to find out what Michael Morville had been up to at the theatre.

* * *

Back at the station, a message from the Residence had been delivered. Archie Clutterbuck required an update on the investigation before he left for official business in Kandy.

De Silva's brow furrowed. He wanted to find Morville as soon as possible but he'd better postpone that. He wondered what the urgency was on Clutterbuck's part. His frown deepened. Was he going to be leant on to bring the investigation to an end? If so, it was proof that the British were at the bottom of this murder. But using the evidence would be as risk free as rolling over the precipice at World's End in a barrel. As the Morris purred along the sunlit road to the Residence, his suspicions, and his apprehension, mounted.

It was past midday when he arrived. Apart from some gardeners working in the shade, no one was about. Today, the pristine white classical portico that fronted the house seemed to have a Roman severity to it: a symbol in stone of Imperial order and power. For a moment, it daunted him.

He swallowed and mustered his resolve. He was becoming fanciful; it wouldn't do. The interview that awaited him was going to need a cool head. He parked the Morris then ran up the steps and rang the bell. The sound pierced his ears like the last trumpet.

'The master is down at the lake, sahib,' said the servant who answered the door. 'Do you need me to show you the way?'

'No, I can find it myself.' He walked round the house and set off across the croquet lawn feeling grumpy. Clutterbuck could spare a morning for his beloved fishing, but he expected other people to jump when he wanted them.

Beyond the croquet lawn, a path through laurels and rhododendrons led to a rougher lawn that sloped down to the lake. Where the water wasn't shaded by overhanging willows, it glittered in the sunshine. On the far side, where the water was deeper, he saw a rowing boat moored at the end of a jetty. Nearby on the bank, Clutterbuck was casting for fish.

De Silva waved as he drew closer and Clutterbuck raised a hand in acknowledgement and put down his rod.

'You're just in time to share a spot of lunch,' he said, but although the tone was affable, his expression was oddly wary. 'The kitchen put me up some sandwiches and pork pies. Mrs Clutterbuck's out for lunch at one of her clubs.'

Two folding chairs and a camp table were already set up in the shade of a tree. Clutterbuck led the way and they sat down. He gestured to the hamper on the table. 'Help yourself. I hope you're hungry.'

The prospect of sandwiches never thrilled de Silva and he expected Jane would have a much more appetising lunch for him at home but, to be polite, he took a triangle of egg and cress.

'Oh, I forgot the drinks. You'll have a beer with me, I hope.'

Before de Silva had a chance to answer, Clutterbuck heaved himself out of his chair and went to the bank. He pulled on a rope that hung down into the water and reeled it in to reveal several bottles of beer tied on at the end. He untied two, carried them dripping to the table and found a bottle opener. The first cap levered off with a pop. A little plume of froth rose to the lip of the bottle and slid down the side. De Silva was no more a fan of beer than he was of sandwiches, but he decided that, in the circumstances, he had better accept the offer.

'Thank you, sir. That's very kind.'

'Not at all.'

Clutterbuck opened the second bottle, took a swig and leant back in his chair. 'Nectar after a hard morning's fishing, eh, de Silva?' A strained silence fell. 'India Pale Ale,' Clutterbuck remarked after a few moments. 'You know the story perhaps? Scotsman by the name of McEwan invented the process. Made him a millionaire. Only beer in the world that travels well to the tropics.'

'I have heard something about it, sir.'

Clutterbuck took a pork pie and gestured to the hamper. 'These aren't bad. Try one. Not quite up to Fortnum and Mason standards but the cooks do their best.'

Taking a pie, de Silva wondered how long it was going to be before the assistant government agent got to the point. The suspense was killing him.

Silence fell again, broken only by the sound of Clutterbuck munching his pork pie. He swallowed the last morsel and wiped his mouth with a napkin. 'Good of you to come at such short notice, de Silva.'

'It wasn't a problem, sir.'

'But I expect you're busy with this blasted Danforth business.'

Already apprehensive, de Silva's mood sank even further.

Clutterbuck shot him an odd look, almost imploring. 'Look, I'll come to the point. I asked you out here today to clear something up. It's dashed tricky. But I hope I can rely on your discretion.'

The words were out before de Silva could stop them.

'I'm sorry, sir, but I will not close down my investigation. If the British government does not like it, then I must ask you to relieve me of my post.'

Clutterbuck stared at him, open mouthed. 'The British government? What has the British government got to do with anything?'

De Silva felt as if he had slid off the nearby bank and was descending irrevocably into deep, muddy waters. 'Alexander Danforth was Irish,' he said awkwardly.

'What of it?' Clutterbuck looked puzzled.

'I understand there is sympathy between the rebels in India and the Irish, and I appreciate this is a difficult time for Britain that they may try to take advantage of. If Danforth was involved in anything underhand on their behalf, anything that might prejudice the peace of Ceylon, I agree he should be brought to justice, but murder is the law of the jungle. I do not want to believe it is the British way.'

He stopped, unsure how to read the expression on Clutterbuck's jowly face. Was it relief or embarrassment?

A sound like the bark of a spotted deer escaped Clutterbuck's throat. De Silva wasn't sure at first whether it was a laugh or an expression of annoyance.

'And I hope you'll believe *me*,' Clutterbuck said solemnly, 'when I assure you that I would never ask you to condone such an action. Entirely between ourselves, I'm afraid there'll almost certainly be bad news from England in the not too distant future.' The flush on his cheeks deepened. 'But no, you're barking up the wrong tree, de Silva. What I have to say has nothing to do with politics. It concerns an entirely different matter.'

CHAPTER 18

'The fact is, the fellow the caretaker told you about – the one he saw lurking outside the theatre – that man was me.'

He paused and de Silva looked at him blankly.

'I trust you to keep this to yourself, de Silva. Not that anything improper occurred, but you know what people are like, and if it came to my wife's ears—' Clutterbuck took out his handkerchief and dabbed his brow. 'Mrs Clutterbuck's a fine woman. She's been my rock through all the years we've been married. I wouldn't want her upset.'

De Silva stared as the assistant government agent rambled on.

'She might not understand. You know how women can be. Least said and all that. It was just I had this damn fool idea about delivering those dratted roses to the stage door myself, like in the old days, but then that bloody caretaker! Poking his nose where it wasn't wanted.'

Slowly, light dawned. The uncharacteristic yellow tie Clutterbuck had worn; the faded yellow roses in Kathleen Danforth's dressing room; the note in the wastepaper basket signed "Bunnikins". Archie Clutterbuck was Bunnikins! De Silva almost choked as he suppressed a gurgle of mirth.

'Yes,' said Clutterbuck uncomfortably. 'It was a very long time ago. I expect you find it hard to imagine. As the years go by, I find it well-nigh impossible myself – but I was a young man once.'

De Silva pulled himself together. 'Believe me, sir, it is a difficulty many of us experience.'

Clutterbuck's face relaxed in an awkward, curiously touching grin. 'But you might not have been such a fool as to lose your head over an old flame, eh?'

'Never having been in the predicament, I can't say, sir.'

'Very diplomatic of you.'

Clutterbuck took a gulp of beer and wiped the froth from his lips.

'I met Kathleen Danforth when I was first in London. I'd grown up in the country. One of those rural backwaters that poets like to rhapsodise about. A Quaker meeting would be livelier. Anyway, an uncle helped me to get my first post in the Colonial Office. I had good prospects, money in my pocket, and I was determined to enjoy life.'

A faraway look came into his eyes and de Silva waited.

'I took to going to the theatre and that was where I saw her. She was playing the juvenile lead in a comedy that was very popular in those days. She was the most beautiful girl I'd ever seen.'

He fell silent and the faraway look returned. De Silva had never suspected that Clutterbuck's bluff, sometimes abrasive, exterior hid a romantic soul. Nervous of stepping out of line, he waited.

'Her name was Kathleen O'Connor then. It was later that Danforth came along. In the meantime, we had a glorious summer, but I think she knew before I did that it wasn't meant to be. A colonial wife needs certain qualities and Mrs Clutterbuck possesses them in abundance. The life wouldn't have suited a woman like Kathleen. Going back to those roses, the incident reminded me, if I needed reminding, that it all worked out for the best and I should be grateful. After my ignominious departure, I found a rickshaw boy to deliver the flowers and went home to the Residence.'

He sniffed vigorously and took another gulp of beer. 'So there you have it, de Silva. No skulduggery and espionage. Just an old fool who should know better.'

CHAPTER 19

Jane wiped her eyes with her handkerchief. 'Poor Archie, I can't help laughing at the thought of him being nicknamed Bunnikins, but it is rather sad too.'

'Why? He said he's happy with Florence now.'

'I'm sure he is, but obviously Kathleen Danforth's arrival stirred up feelings that hadn't entirely gone away.'

'Yes. As you say, poor old Archie.'

Jane rested her chin on her hand. 'He might have been quite attractive as a young man, you know. He's not bad looking and I expect he was a lot slimmer than he is now. He's very charming when he wants to be too.'

'I'll defer to your opinion on that,' de Silva said with a laugh. 'No, to be fair, there have been many times when I've found him pleasant company. Anyway, we must forget all about this business with Kathleen Danforth. I promised him I would be discreet.'

'Absolutely. It would be very unkind to embarrass him, or Florence.'

De Silva raised an eyebrow. 'To say nothing of the effect on my job.'

He yawned. 'There's been far too much excitement for one morning. I might have a little nap before I go back to the station.'

'A very good plan, dear.'

* * *

At least he had one less suspect to deal with, he thought later, on the drive into town. At the station, he saw Prasanna going in the front door and called out to him. The sergeant turned and hurried over.

'Good news, sir! I found the place at last. The owner of the shop had to go back to his village for a few days because his father was sick and the person he left in charge did not serve the lady, but the owner remembered her. A British lady, tall with dark hair and a fierce expression. She brought a key and wanted a copy cut straight away. He thought it was strange at the time. British ladies do not usually run their own errands in Nuala, but he did not like to ask questions. He was afraid.'

De Silva's eyebrows shot up. It had to be Olive Reilly. The question was, who had she been helping or was she acting alone? And if so, how had she got out of the theatre unobserved?

Then a new possibility dawned on him. It might end in nothing, but that bar in the theatre foyer, had he missed something there? On his usual principle of no stone unturned, perhaps he should have taken the trouble to investigate it.

'I'd better get up to the Crown Hotel. I want to know what Kathleen Danforth's maid has to say for herself. I think she must be the one who had the key cut. Meanwhile, I'd like you to visit the theatre. Find the caretaker and tell him to show you that bar in the foyer.'

Prasanna looked puzzled. 'Why, sir?'

'There may be something that will help us. How many ways to get to it in particular.'

'Right, sir.'

Prasanna hesitated. 'Will you arrest the maid, sir?'

De Silva considered this. Kathleen Danforth probably

wouldn't be happy about Reilly being arrested and he still wasn't sure what her own part in the business was. He should really detain them both and that risked causing problems with Archie. At the very least, he needed to be warned.

'Not yet. I must put in a call to the Residence before I do anything else.'

Sitting at his desk waiting for the call to go through, he drummed his fingers. This was not likely to be an easy conversation. For once, he had the advantage over Clutterbuck, but the concern he had already shown for his old flame was unlikely to have diminished.

The telephone shrilled and he lifted the receiver.

'Clutterbuck here.' The assistant government agent's voice sounded wary. When de Silva had finished explaining what Prasanna had discovered, there was a long silence.

'I can't prevent you from questioning Kathleen,' Clutterbuck said at last. 'But you won't find the Reilly woman at the Crown. Miss Watson's disappeared too. I've just had David Hebden on in a terrible state. She promised to meet him at the club for lunch and never turned up. Reaction's a bit over the top if you ask me, she might have simply changed her mind, but he seems very keen, poor chap. On the other hand, Reilly going missing is strange.'

A feeling of foreboding came over de Silva.

'I've postponed my business in Kandy,' Clutterbuck added. 'I'll meet you at the Crown in half an hour.'

* * *

'I don't know what to think, Inspector.'

Kathleen Danforth's face was pale but there were dark shadows around her eyes. 'Olive has been acting out of character for several days. Normally, she never makes mistakes.

In fact, she always insists on doing far more than she needs because she doesn't trust other people to do things properly. But the day before yesterday, she singed the lace on one of my nightgowns with the iron. She broke a very expensive bottle of perfume too.'

She gave de Silva an imploring look. 'Olive hasn't been with me for very long, Inspector, but she's a good woman in spite of her off-putting manner and I've grown to like her very much. I'm mystified, indeed horrified, by the idea that she wished my husband harm. She must have known the grief his death would cause me. Please find her. I'm sure there will be an innocent explanation for everything.'

She put a slim hand to her throat. 'What if she's had an accident? She may be in desperate need of help.'

De Silva didn't have such faith in Olive Reilly's innocence but he caught the glance Clutterbuck gave him and he kept his views to himself. On the other hand, he was inclined to believe Kathleen Danforth was telling the truth.

'We'll do our best, ma'am.'

'Indeed we will. You must try not to worry,' soothed Clutterbuck.

'I can't think how I'll manage in the meantime,' Kathleen said with a sigh. 'At a time like this, I can't bear anything else to go wrong.'

'I'll speak to the manager here and arrange for them to give you a maid to help out until she returns.'

Kathleen gave him a wistful smile. 'You're very kind, my dear.'

'Right, you'd better get straight onto it, de Silva,' said Clutterbuck as they left the hotel. 'Any help the Residence can give, you know you need only ask.'

'Thank you, sir. I'd be grateful if your driver would take a message to my men at the police station. I want to stop off at the hotel where the rest of the company are staying. It will be interesting to know when any of them last saw the missing ladies.'

'Good plan, should've thought of that myself.'

In the lobby, de Silva wrote a note to Prasanna and Nadar instructing them to begin a new search. As he licked the envelope and sealed it, he felt rather sorry for them both. They had worn out a lot of shoe leather over the last few days. Still, in his own early days in Colombo, coming home dusty and footsore hadn't been an unusual occurrence.

* * *

The Nuala Hotel was a sprawling bungalow set in far more modest grounds than the Crown. It looked as if it might once have been the home of a planter. The front door was closed so de Silva pressed the bell and waited. Eventually, a servant came to the door and told him that Michael Morville was the only one in, and was in the garden.

De Silva followed the servant's directions along a weedy path that led round the side of the bungalow, past an ornamental pond where a pair of mallards drifted disconsolately between mats of water lilies, and onto an expanse of thirsty lawn. A lone flowerbed displayed spindly roses and, in the far left-hand corner, in the shade of a clump of banana trees, Michael Morville dozed in a deck chair. He wore a crumpled linen jacket and a panama hat tilted over his face. His legs were encased in a pair of ancient cricket flannels.

A twig cracked under de Silva's foot as he approached and Morville tipped up the brim of his hat, blinking in the sunshine. 'Why Inspector! To what do I owe the pleasure?'

De Silva decided to proceed with caution. 'It's a routine enquiry. I'd be grateful if you would tell me your movements in the last couple of days.'

'Let me see... The day before yesterday I was here all day – the staff will vouch for that. Yesterday, I was here in the morning, but after lunch, I went to the barbers at the Crown.' He rubbed a hand over his chin. 'Afterwards, I took a rickshaw up to the theatre. I still had a few belongings there I wanted to collect. Not that I enjoy visiting the dismal place after what happened.' He smiled ruefully. 'Does that help you, Inspector?'

De Silva thanked him. The information would be easy enough to verify.

'If you want to speak to the others, you'd do best to look for Sheridan and Raikes in town at the Nuala Club. It appears to have become their second home.'

The place was known to de Silva. The Nuala Club was frequented by the lower echelons of colonial society who failed to gain entry to the hallowed portals of the Empire Club.

'What about Mr Mayne?'

'Propping up the bar there too, I expect.'

Morville raised an eyebrow. 'Although there's not much love lost between him and the other two.'

'And Mr Crichton?'

Morville shrugged. 'Who knows what poor old Charlie gets up to? He's never fitted in really. It's always surprised me that Alexander kept him on.' He gave de Silva a penetrating look. 'You mustn't take too much notice of what he says, you know. Particularly about Raikes and Sheridan. Raikes enjoys baiting him and Sheridan's never made a secret of the fact he's got no time for him.'

'One more thing. Have either Mrs Danforth's maid or Miss Watson been here in the last few days?'

'Olive?' He chuckled. 'I doubt she'd be interested in our company, nor would Miss Watson for that matter.'

'Well, thank you, sir. If you should see either of them, I'd be grateful if you'd send word to the police station.'

Morville frowned. 'You have cause to be worried about them?'

'Nothing's certain yet, sir. There may be a simple explanation, but Olive Reilly's not been seen for several days and Miss Watson missed a lunch and hasn't been heard from. I would like to know their whereabouts.'

* * *

When he returned to the station, there was no sign of Prasanna or Nadar, presumably they were still busy searching. But there was a note from Prasanna that gave him a jolt. There was indeed a side door behind the foyer bar as the caretaker had said. It couldn't be opened from the outside but inside, all that secured it were two strong bolts. With only a little more exploration of the area behind the bar, Prasanna had also found a passage that ran parallel to the auditorium stalls. At the end of it was another door, unlocked but opening only a few inches.

Picturing his young sergeant's earnest face, de Silva smiled as he read Prasanna's account of how he'd had to speak firmly to the caretaker and old Prathiv before they would help. At last, with them all putting their shoulders to the door, the obstruction, which turned out to be a cupboard, moved and they found themselves in a storeroom. It was one of the ones adjacent to the men's dressing rooms that de Silva and Nadar had already searched. It was only then that Prathiv remembered that the route had, in the old days, been used to take drinks to the actors in intervals.

De Silva let out a low whistle, then scowled. Far from being the fount of all knowledge about the theatre he was touted as, that forgetful old fool Prathiv had been no help. He was cross with himself too. Admittedly, this case had been frustrating, and he'd been distracted by his suspicions about the British, but he shouldn't have let that deflect him from observing his golden rule.

'It does seem very strange, Olive Reilly disappearing like this,' said Jane when he telephoned to fill her in on the latest developments and warn her he might be late home that evening. 'Have you told anyone apart from Archie and Kathleen Danforth about the key?'

'No. At the moment, I'm not sure who I can trust.'

'Very wise, dear. This passage Prasanna's discovered certainly opens up more possibilities, doesn't it?'

'Indeed it does.'

'I expect Emerald Watson will turn up soon. Maybe she forgot the lunch appointment. I hope Doctor Hebden isn't too anxious. I find it hard to credit that Emerald and Olive Reilly would be conspirators.'

'Why do you say that?'

'Peggy Appleby – you know she's become very friendly with Emerald – told me Emerald wasn't keen on Olive Reilly. Far too controlling and a bad influence on Kathleen Danforth.'

'With respect to Mrs Appleby, she hasn't known Miss Watson for long, and it's possible she was being deliberately misled.'

'I suppose that's true, but until I see proof, I won't believe it. She seems such a delightful young woman and that nice Doctor Hebden is so taken with her.'

'I've gathered that, and I sincerely hope he won't have to be disillusioned. Anyway, I'd better get on with the search. Don't wait dinner for me.'

* * *

Jane had finished dinner and was reading in the drawing room by the time he returned home.

'You poor thing, you must be ravenous,' she said, putting down her book. 'I told Cook to keep something warm for you.'

186

He flopped into his chair. 'No need, I ate at the Nuala Club when I went to look for the other men.'

'Did you find them?'

'Raikes and Mayne were there but no sign of Crichton or Sheridan. They said they hadn't seen either of them recently.'

Jane frowned. 'I don't like the sound of that.'

'Neither do I, but I've called off the search for tonight. We start again first thing.'

* * *

The ringing of the telephone in the hall roused him from sleep. The bedroom was still in shadow but the rim of pale gold at the hem of the curtains showed it was after dawn. Beside him, Jane stirred. 'What is it? Was that the telephone?'

'Yes, I'd better get up.'

He swung his legs out of bed and pushed his feet into his slippers. He was reaching for his paisley robe when there was a soft knock at the door. He hurried to open it. The servant who greeted him looked half asleep. 'A call from Doctor Hebden, sahib.'

De Silva strode past him and went to the telephone. He listened for a few moments and gave a short reply then put down the receiver.

'Shanti? What's happened?' Jane had donned her dressing gown and come into the hall.

'A body's been found in the town lake. A couple of local men notified Hebden, and Archie Clutterbuck's also been told.'

'Oh my goodness!'

'I'd better get down there straight away.'

CHAPTER 20

With very little traffic on the road, he reached the lake in record time. Its silky waters were like liquid mother-of-pearl in the early morning light. As the noise of the Morris's engine broke the stillness, a purple heron rose from the reeds and flapped away on its huge wings.

De Silva scanned the grassy banks and saw a huddle of people at the end of the lake. He put the Morris into low gear and drove slowly towards them. As he came near, he glimpsed one of the official cars from the Residence, almost hidden by a clump of trees, and beside it, the dark-red Austin 7 belonging to David Hebden. Small colourful boats, their prows painted with the magic eye to ward off evil, were drawn up on the bank. Coconut-fibre baskets shimmered with the night's scaly, iridescent catch.

Clutterbuck and Hebden looked up as he approached. The fishermen with them muttered among themselves. In the centre of the circle lay the body of a woman: Olive Reilly. Water from her heavy black clothes pooled around her; her sodden hair hung limply to her shoulders. Her face, already showing signs of bloating, was as white as blanched almonds, but there were livid patches on her sharp cheekbones as if she had clumsily applied rouge before she died.

'These men say they saw nothing,' said Hebden. 'They were fishing out in the middle of the lake most of the night. I don't think she's been in the water long, maybe only a few hours. The body had almost come to the surface when the men saw it, but then it wouldn't take long for the gases to build up in this warm water.'

'It's shallow here too,' added Clutterbuck.

'Do you think she was murdered, Doctor Hebden?'

Hebden shook his head. 'It looks more like suicide. There were no bruises or other signs of blows on the body.'

De Silva knelt beside the motionless figure. The skin on the palms of her hands and her fingertips was already wrinkled but they weren't scratched and there was no mud or water weed under her fingernails. Olive Reilly hadn't fought for her life as its end approached.

He stood up and spoke to the men in Tamil. 'You're sure you saw nothing? Don't be afraid to tell me. You won't be in any trouble.'

The only response was a series of shaken heads.

'We're wasting time,' growled Clutterbuck. 'We won't learn anything here. Hebden, you'd better arrange for the body to be removed to the hospital morgue. Will you travel with me, de Silva? I'm afraid we'll have to take on the unpleasant duty of breaking the news to Kathleen Danforth.'

A few moments later, the official car drew away. Archie was right that it would be an unpleasant task, but at least, de Silva reflected, they were getting somewhere.

* * *

When they were shown into Kathleen Danforth's suite at the Crown, however, it was immediately apparent that their job was already half done.

She held out the letter she had been reading. 'It's from Olive.' There was a catch in her voice. 'I presume you've come to tell me she's dead.'

'I'm very sorry, Kathleen.' Clutterbuck went over to her and took her hands. 'I wish I could have spared you another shock.'

'It's not your fault.'

'May I see the letter, ma'am?' asked de Silva.

Wordlessly, she gave him the piece of paper.

'As you'll see, Inspector, it was Frank Sheridan who killed my poor husband and Olive helped him. I never realised she even liked Frank, let alone loved him. She says she would have done anything for him, but then he betrayed her.'

Clutterbuck looked bemused. 'But why would Sheridan want your husband dead? I thought they were old friends.'

De Silva looked up from reading the letter. 'According to Reilly, it wasn't as simple as that, sir. Sheridan told her he'd lent Mr Danforth a large sum of money when the company started out. He trusted him to return it if ever he asked for it, and he did on several occasions, but Mr Danforth always said it was the wrong time.'

Kathleen Danforth made an impatient gesture. 'I don't believe a word of that. Alexander never mentioned it and I expect Frank had a grossly inflated idea of how much he was owed if anything at all.'

'Your husband may have kept money troubles from you, ma'am. Not wanting to worry you.'

'I doubt it,' Kathleen said acerbically. 'Olive says there that Frank spun her a story about becoming suspicious Alexander was cheating him. He persuaded her it had to be true with the money Alexander was spending, especially the air fare to England for Emerald's twenty-first birthday celebration. Not that either of them knew that was the reason for the journey.'

De Silva nodded. 'It must have cost a large amount.'

'It did. I should know as I paid for it.'

Clutterbuck and de Silva looked at her with surprise.

'Alexander never had any money,' she went on. 'Whenever the company was in trouble, I bailed him out.'

She paced to the window and swung round sharply; the light falling on her hair turned it to fire. 'I only wanted Alexander to be happy. How was I to know that buying him the ticket to England would precipitate disaster? Or that Olive would help Frank Sheridan to steal from us? Damn him. No wonder he came on to her for months. He could never have done it without her.'

'How much did they take?' asked Clutterbuck frowning.

'Thousands of pounds. In bearer bonds.'

De Silva recalled a case he had worked on in Colombo that had involved the theft of bearer bonds. The financial instruments had the advantage that they could be easily cashed anywhere in the world. Obviously, that would suit the Danforths on their travels, but the disadvantage was that as the bonds were issued in the name of no specific person, they were like cash and vulnerable to theft and fraud, as had been the problem in the Colombo affair.

Clutterbuck grimaced. 'I'll move heaven and earth if I have to and we'll get them back.'

'If only you could bring Alexander back as well. And poor Olive. She's more to be pitied than blamed. It was cruel the way Frank Sheridan deceived her.' Her voice caught in her throat and she stepped out onto the balcony. Both men left her alone to recover her composure.

De Silva reached the end of the letter and spoke quietly to Clutterbuck. 'Reilly writes that Sheridan begged her to help him get his revenge on Danforth. He also told her he wanted the money back so they could go away together and have a good life. He persuaded her it was best not to reveal their relationship. He said Danforth would try to have her dismissed for sure before they could carry out their plan. He wouldn't want her to be in Sheridan's confidence when she was becoming closer to Mrs Danforth. At first, Reilly only agreed to help him steal the bonds, but, in the end, he convinced her that they should kill Danforth as well or they'd never be free of him.'

Kathleen returned, in control of herself again. 'When it was over, she realised the full horror of what she'd helped him do but she knew she had to hold her nerve. She planned for them to stay in Nuala, hoping the fuss would die down and they could make their escape undetected. That was when Frank told her she'd served her purpose. She was distraught.'

She paused. 'Poor Olive decided the only thing to do was to end her life,' she finished quietly.

And, thought de Silva, she would also have realised that in exposing Sheridan's crime, she would incriminate herself as his accomplice and probably hang anyway.

He folded the letter. 'May I take this, ma'am? It will be needed in evidence.'

'Of course, Inspector. Where will you look for Frank?'

'I'm not sure yet, ma'am, but I'll do my utmost to find him.'

'What about Emerald?'

'We've no evidence she had any part in all this,' said Clutterbuck. 'I'm sure she'll turn up soon.'

Kathleen nodded but de Silva was less sure. He didn't like coincidences and he had a nasty feeling that Emerald Watson was in danger. He also had a feeling there was more to this than the letter had revealed.

* * *

'I didn't want to cause Kathleen any more distress by pro-longing the interview, so you'd better tell me now what else was in the letter,' said Clutterbuck. 'Does it explain how they did it?'

'Yes, it's clear that once he'd revealed his true colours, Reilly didn't want Sheridan to get away with his crime, so she put everything that happened in her letter. Sheridan wielded them, but the scissors that killed Danforth were hers. She had a second pair in case I insisted on seeing the ones in her work basket. She was also the one who laid the groundwork. She watched the caretaker and very soon realised he was unreliable. When he wasn't around, she had no trouble taking the key I mentioned to you, then she put it back unnoticed once she'd had a spare one cut.'

They reached the place in the Crown's car park where the official car waited in the shade. 'I'll give you a lift back to your own car,' said Clutterbuck.

'Thank you, sir.'

As the black Daimler set off, Clutterbuck leant forward and made sure the screen between them and his driver was firmly shut. 'Go on.'

'The caretaker was in his booth that evening so Sheridan took the key for the yard that led to the cellar. He operated the stage trap to get up on the stage and Reilly helped him out.'

'Lucky he knew how to use the thing.'

De Silva groaned as his mind flashed back to one of his early conversations with the caretaker. 'I remember now. The caretaker told me Sheridan went down to the cellar with Raikes and the mechanic from Gopallawa Motors. That gave him the opportunity to familiarise himself with how the thing worked and the chance to observe which key was used and describe it to Reilly.'

'You can hardly be blamed for not making the connection at that stage, de Silva. He was going to use the thing for his role in the play.'

'Thank you, sir.'

'But wasn't there a risk someone would see him? Presumably there would be blood on his clothes?'

'Reilly must have helped him to change and destroyed the soiled clothing.'

Another memory came back to him of the powerful smell of perfume in Olive Reilly's workroom the first time he visited it. He hadn't noticed it being so strong the second time he went there. Was that where she had burnt the clothes, splashing perfume around to mask the smell? Perhaps the contents of the expensive bottle of perfume she told Kathleen she had broken.

Clutterbuck scratched his chin. 'There's one thing I don't follow. How did Sheridan get out of the building with the caretaker around?'

'I'm coming to that, sir.'

'Right.'

De Silva felt gratified at the ease with which the assistant government agent was persuaded to be patient. He listened, occasionally nodding, as de Silva explained about Prasanna finding the passage and the door behind the foyer bar.

'Why didn't Kathleen notice Reilly was up to something that afternoon?'

'Reilly gave her a drink laced with a dose of the same barbiturate she had slipped into Danforth's brandy earlier in the day.'

'I see. Well, it's a pity Reilly didn't leave us any clues about where we'll find this fellow Sheridan.'

'A great pity,' de Silva agreed gloomily. He hoped that when they did, if Emerald Watson had been taken hostage, it wouldn't be too late to save her.

CHAPTER 21

'I'll put in a call to David Hebden when I get back to the Residence,' said Clutterbuck. 'The poor fellow's very anxious about Miss Watson and I expect he'll want to join in the search. It seems there's an understanding between them, at least so my wife informs me.'

'Mine too, sir. Might it be better if I speak to him then we can co-ordinate our efforts?'

'Good thinking. If it helps, I'll let you have the other official car and a driver.'

'Thank you.'

Clutterbuck rubbed his forehead wearily. 'Troubled times, de Silva; troubled times. On top of all this, I heard last night that the King has finally resolved to abdicate. The legalities will be finalised immediately and a public announcement made. In a few days, it will be all change and his brother will be king. I can't help but feel the Empire has lost a fine man.'

'I'm sorry to hear it, sir.'

They reached the lake and de Silva started up the Morris and set off for the police station. There, he telephoned the hospital. Hebden was still there.

'The bastard!' he spluttered, jettisoning his customary measured tones, after de Silva brought him up to date.

'It's not a foregone conclusion that Sheridan has her.'

'Where else can she be?'

197

De Silva had to admit he didn't know.

'He wants her as a hostage, I'm sure of it. Well, what do we do now? We've got to find her before she's harmed. When I catch up with him—'

He didn't finish the sentence and de Silva realised he was struggling to master his emotions.

'A reward, that's what we need,' Hebden started again. 'And posters up all over town.'

'Do you have a photograph of Miss Watson?'

'No.'

Hebden's voice was flat with despair.

'There were photographs at the theatre,' said de Silva with a flash of inspiration. 'They might still be there. I'll drive up straight away.'

'I'll follow you and we can decide what to do next.'

Hurrying out to the Morris, de Silva looked at his wristwatch. The hospital was on the far side of town from the theatre so Hebden would probably be about half an hour behind him. With luck, by the time the doctor arrived, he would have found a poster they could take down to the printers.

He had only gone as far as the post office when he realised he hadn't brought his gun. He turned in the forecourt under the clock tower and went back. In his office, he buckled on his holster and tucked the Webley into it. Rearranging his uniform jacket to conceal the bulge, he patted the lapel; it was as well to be prepared.

Intent on making up for lost time, he didn't think twice about the silver-grey Lagonda he had glimpsed before he turned back to the station. Then all at once, like the first drops of water falling after a day heavy with the promise of rain, it came to him – the last person he had seen driving a silver-grey Lagonda round Nuala was Alexander Danforth. It was highly unlikely there would be two models of such a fine car in a small town.

He searched his memory. He hadn't noticed the car at the theatre. Wouldn't Danforth have driven up there that evening?

As soon as he cleared the bazaar, he speeded up and, ten minutes later, the theatre's grandiose façade came into view. He parked the Morris a little way off and made his way quietly to the back of the building. The silver-grey Lagonda was parked in the yard by the stage door. If Sheridan was the driver, de Silva marvelled at his coolness.

At first, he thought he was imagining it, but as he passed the car, it seemed to rock slightly. He went closer and heard muffled noises as if someone inside was struggling. The noises grew louder and more frantic; now he realised they came from the boot. He tried to open it but it was locked. He put his lips close to the searing metal. 'I'm going to get you out, but I'll have to shoot off the lock. Keep as far away as you can.'

He pulled the Webley from its holster, put the muzzle of the gun up against the lock and pulled the trigger. The bullet tore into the metal with a blast that split the air. His ears throbbed as the sound reverberated around the courtyard. Flinging up the lid was like opening the door of an oven. Filled with terror, Emerald Watson's hazel eyes stared at him out of the gloom inside. She was gagged and her hands and feet were bound with tape. Her hair clung to her streaming face.

Quickly he lifted her out and carried her to a patch of shade. She was limp and floppy as a rag doll, but to his relief, as soon as he removed the gag, she took a huge gulp of air and spoke.

'Frank Sheridan,' she gasped. 'He's gone crazy.'

'It was Sheridan who did this to you?' He hurried to release her hands and feet.

She nodded then burst into tears. 'Thank God you came. It was so horrible… I thought I was going to die.'

He smoothed her hair from her face. Her skin was burning to the touch. 'It's alright, you're safe now. Do you know what Sheridan's after here?'

'Money. He left some money hidden in the theatre with forged passports for the two of us. He said we'd leave Ceylon together and he'd kill me if I tried to run away. He kept calling me Polly. Inspector de Silva, Polly was my mother's name. I don't understand what's going on.'

Polly? For a moment, de Silva didn't understand either. Then he remembered what Morville had said. Did Sheridan mean Polly Devlin, the woman he had loved but who had preferred Alexander Danforth to him? But she had died long ago. Then everything became clear. Morville had also said that Emerald looked rather like Polly. The young woman's resemblance to her mother must have tipped Sheridan over the edge. He believed Polly had come back to him. The man wasn't just dangerous, he was deranged.

Emerald froze. 'That noise! He's coming back.'

De Silva glanced at the stage door. 'Not yet, and don't be afraid, I'll deal with him, but if he's anywhere nearby, he will have heard that shot so we've no time to lose. David Hebden will be here in a few minutes. Will you be alright on your own until he arrives?'

'I… I think so,' she stammered, her expression belying her words.

He went to the driver's door. 'Sheridan can't have been thinking straight. He left the keys. Can you drive a car, Miss Watson?'

'My father let me drive this one once or twice, although it wasn't on the road.'

'I'll start the engine, then all you have to do is steer. Do you remember how the brakes work?'

'Yes.'

The engine growled into life and he slid out of the seat and held the door for her. 'Remember, foot gently on the accelerator as you ease off the clutch. Drive very slowly and stay in first gear. You only need to go a short way until you're out of sight, then pull over to the side of the road and wait for David Hebden. Don't forget to put the gear in neutral before you turn off the engine.'

She nodded and climbed into the driving seat. As she gripped the steering wheel, her knuckles were white. 'Shall I start now, Inspector?' she asked shakily.

There was a grinding noise and the car jerked forward and stalled. She let out a cry of alarm. 'Oh, I can't do it!'

'Yes, you can. Try again.'

Her small white teeth nipped her bottom lip. This time the car edged forward.

'That's it! Now slowly, and don't forget to stop as soon as you're out of sight of the theatre.'

The stage door creaked open when he turned the handle. There was no sign of the caretaker. Another indication that he wasn't as devoted to his duty as he tried to make out. He hadn't even bothered to secure the place. Unless Sheridan had tied him up too, but finding out would have to wait.

The lobby was a furnace. Beads of sweat formed on de Silva's forehead and his collar chafed the back of his neck.

He decided to search the dressing rooms on Sheridan's side first. As he crept along the right-hand passage, his hand closed around the reassuring metal of his gun. There was no sign of Sheridan on the ground floor. He went to the staircase and hesitated for a moment on the first step, listening for the creak of floorboards or the sound of a door opening or closing upstairs. Silence. Had Sheridan found another way out? If he had, he would soon know that Emerald had escaped. What would he do then? Come back inside to try and find who had released her, or leave the theatre in pursuit? De Silva was confident that before Sheridan had time to find her, she would be safe with David Hebden.

Suddenly, his stomach lurched. Footsteps approached

the top of the stairs and, the next moment, a figure disturbed the shadows. He glimpsed Frank Sheridan's pale, angry face and raised his gun. 'Stop there! Frank Sheridan, I'm arresting you for the murder of Alexander Danforth and the kidnapping of Emerald Watson.'

In the half darkness, Sheridan's wolfish smile gave him a satanic air. 'If you think I murdered Alexander, Inspector, what makes you so sure I won't kill you?'

De Silva took another step up the stairs. 'I don't want to shoot you, sir. Please come quietly.'

Sheridan sneered. 'That line would disgrace the most pedestrian of crime dramas, Inspector.'

If it was an attempt to throw him off balance, Sheridan was wasting his time.

'Just come down, sir. I won't ask you again.'

'How right you are, Inspector.'

Almost too fast for de Silva to see what was happening, metal gleamed and there was the crack of a gunshot. The bullet ricocheted off the stair rail taking a lump of wood with it. De Silva returned fire and the gun flew from Sheridan's hand, clattering away out of reach of them both. Sheridan took off down the passageway.

Gun in hand, de Silva ran up the stairs and followed. He was just in time to see Sheridan disappear through a door and slam it behind him. De Silva waited for a moment to catch his breath then turned the handle. His mouth was dry as he went in.

He didn't recognise the room. It must have been one that Nadar checked. It was empty, but a small section of flooring had been removed in one corner; presumably very recently or Nadar would have noticed and mentioned it. A hiding place for the stolen bearer bonds perhaps?

A rush of air behind him made him swing round. Sheridan's fist slammed into his ribs doubling him up with pain. He dropped the Webley and Sheridan made a grab for it. Winded, de Silva tottered as the actor took aim.

The trigger clicked, and clicked again but the gun had jammed. With a shout of anger, Sheridan tossed it away then barged past de Silva and ran. Trying to ignore the pain in his ribs, de Silva gave chase.

Sheridan reached the far end of the corridor and de Silva saw him run up another staircase, this time a much narrower one. The gap between them decreased as he hurtled through a door and into a props room. De Silva arrived in time to see him seize a rapier that lay on a table and unsheathe it. He recognised the weapon Sheridan had used when he played Laertes and fought Hamlet in the last act of the play.

The blade gleamed. De Silva only just got out of the way in time as, with a howl like a banshee, Sheridan lunged. Desperately, de Silva evaded the blow. Looking around for some way of defending himself, he saw a plaster bust of an ancient Roman and grabbed it. With all the force he could muster, he hurled it at Sheridan but the actor side-stepped just in time. The bust smashed into the wall behind him and disintegrated. His head reeling, he tried to control his voice. 'Give up, Sheridan. Olive Reilly has confessed. The game's over.'

Sheridan bared his teeth in a ghastly simulacrum of a smile. 'Olive Reilly! I suppose the skinny old bitch told you we were in love. What a joke! When I told her I had no more need of her, she was pathetic.' His voice took on a whiny quality. 'Oh Frank, don't leave me. You promised we'd be together.' His lip curled. 'I should have cut her throat then and be done with it.'

De Silva saw how the actor's dark eyes glittered and a chill went through him. The man was even more dangerous than he had anticipated. What was worse, he, de Silva, was unarmed. He backed away, fumbling at the surfaces he came to for anything he might use to knock the rapier out of Sheridan's hand, but before he had any luck, Sheridan lunged once more. De Silva threw the only object he had time to reach, an embroidered cushion, at the flashing blade and it vanished in a storm of feathers. Exhausted and almost senseless, he waited for Sheridan to strike a third time, but Sheridan stepped back, a strange expression on his face.

'The only woman for me has always been Polly,' he said softly. 'And now we can be together.'

De Silva quailed as he realised he had been right about Sheridan. Digging into his memory for what experience had taught him about handling this kind of situation, he forced himself to stay calm. Speak quietly. Win the man's confidence. Don't gainsay him until you have control of the situation.

Tentatively, he stretched out a hand. 'It's alright, Frank. I want to help you. Why don't you put your weapon down? We'll find Polly together and then we can talk.'

Sheridan hesitated and de Silva felt a surge of hope. The rapier pointed to the floor and misery and confusion contorted the actor's face. 'Polly,' he mumbled. 'I have to go to her. She needs me.'

'Of course she does,' de Silva said gently. 'And you'll be together soon. Just give me the rapier.'

Stiffening, Sheridan gave him a suspicious look. 'You know where she is, do you? If you're trying to take her away from me, it won't work.'

'Of course not, Frank. You belong together. I know that.'

For a moment, Sheridan looked disconcerted then he rallied, gimlet-eyed.

'You're lying. You want to keep us apart, just like Alexander did. That's why he had to die, and now you're going to die too.'

He lunged and a stinging pain seared de Silva's right arm. Looking down, he saw the sleeve was in tatters and blood was rapidly soaking the torn fabric. His vision blurred, but he forced himself to say upright and dodge Sheridan's next thrust. He longed to hear rescuers' footsteps but there was only the macabre hiss of Sheridan's swingeing strokes and the thump of his own heartbeat. Soon, his back was to a short staircase that he recognised with dismay. The edge of the first step bruised his shin as he stumbled. He righted himself but his strength was failing fast. He was trapped. Inexorably, Sheridan forced him upward, one agonising step at a time.

As they emerged into the flies, Sheridan slashed at a rope and a tattered curtain gave way, plummeting thirty feet to the ground with a heart-stopping thud, releasing as it did so a cloud of ancient dust that clogged de Silva's nostrils and almost blinded him. Wiping it away with the back of his free hand, he tried to stand his ground but it was over. His head seemed detached from his body; his legs gave way and, arms flailing, he fought to keep his balance. Sheridan advanced one more step. Smiling, he put the tip of his rapier to de Silva's chest.

The ground rushed up as de Silva fell. In the split second before darkness engulfed him, he imagined that he saw once more the fateful words written on the mirror in Danforth's blood: *the rest is silence.*

* * *

Born on the dark wings of everlasting night, he found himself on a high tower. Iron frost gripped the stone walls and battlements. An icy pavement bucked and twisted beneath his feet. A figure armoured in leather and chain mail glided towards him out of the mist, but de Silva passed through it, smelling decay and sour breath. The phantom had Frank Sheridan's face.

Cold: he had never imagined such cold existed. Cold

that made his eyelashes and brows rigid and his face and fingers throb with pain. He tottered to the parapet and stared down into a vast whiteness. Flurries of snowflakes struck him in the face. He tried to bat them away but they were too dense. His lungs were bursting as he fought for breath.

Then silence and the dark.

CHAPTER 22

'Shanti! Oh Shanti! Thank goodness! You're back.'

Jane took his hand and bent to kiss his cheek. He touched the place. 'I can feel you,' he said wonderingly. 'But tell me you're real.'

She gave a shaky laugh. 'Of course I'm real, dear. And so are you.'

'What happened?'

'You were very lucky. When you fell off the walkway, you landed on a bed that had been set up on stage ready for the next production. If it hadn't been for the fact that you bounced off it onto the hard floor, you might have been hardly injured at all.'

'How long have I been unconscious?'

She looked at the clock on the wall. 'I'm not quite sure, but it's been nearly six hours since you were found. The longest hours of my life.'

'Where am I?'

'You're in hospital, dear.'

He tried to struggle to a sitting position but fell back. 'Arggh! My arm!'

'You must lie still, dear. The cut was a deep one. Doctor Hebden had to put a lot of stitches in.'

Looking down, de Silva saw that the offending arm was swathed in bandages. He groaned. 'Where's Sheridan?'

'Arrested. Since Emerald Watson drove off with the

Lagonda, he was stranded and didn't get far. He was spotted by Doctor Hebden and you won't be surprised to learn that *he* was determined to get his man. I must say, everyone was very impressed with the way Emerald managed to cope with such a powerful vehicle. Peggy Appleby said she didn't even know Emerald could drive.'

De Silva smiled. 'She's a fast learner.'

Jane gave him a reproving look. 'Did you have something to do with it, Shanti?'

'I may have done.'

'She might have caused an accident, you know.'

'In the circumstances, that was the least of my worries. I told her to go very slowly, and anyway, no harm was done.'

There was a knock at the door and David Hebden came in.

'Ah, I'm glad to see that my patient is awake.'

He came to the bed, took de Silva's pulse, and listened to his chest with a stethoscope. When he was done with that, he produced a small flashlight and turned it on. 'Head up and stay still. Try not to blink.'

De Silva waited while Hebden shone the light into both of his eyes. 'Most satisfactory,' Hebden said cheerfully when he had finished. 'You're a very fortunate man.'

'I don't wish to be ungrateful, Doctor Hebden, but I would like to go home as soon as possible.'

'Naturally. Let's say tomorrow, all being well. I'd like to keep you in overnight in case you have a relapse, although I don't anticipate trouble.'

He looked at Jane. 'I rely on you to keep him in order, Mrs de Silva. Once he's home, he needs to rest for a week at least.'

Jane smiled. 'I'll make sure of it. How is Miss Watson?'

'Recovering well from her ordeal, thanks to your husband. She's staying with the Applebys for the moment.'

'Good. I'm sure Peggy will look after her excellently.'

'Well, I'd better be off and see my other patients. I'll be back in the morning.'

The door closed behind him and de Silva scowled. 'Rest for a whole week?'

'You'll do as you're told, dear,' said Jane firmly.

'Humph.'

'Anyway, everything's under control with Sheridan in custody, and Archie Clutterbuck has recovered the bearer bonds.'

'That must be a relief to Mrs Danforth.'

'I'm sure it is. At least she won't want for money.' She rested her chin on one hand. 'The financial arrangement between her and her husband did sound a strange one. One can only assume she used her money to keep the upper hand.'

'Drip feeding it to him when she thought she needed to, do you mean?'

'Yes. Perhaps the aeroplane tickets and the luxuries like the Lagonda were to make up for demanding he didn't tell anyone about Emerald.'

'Maybe.'

'But we'll never know. It's hardly the kind of question one can ask.'

'Quite.'

His stomach gave a low rumble. 'Do you think there's anything to eat in this place? I'm hungry.'

Jane smiled and smoothed the hair from his forehead. 'Good. I'm sure I can find something suitable.'

CHAPTER 23

A few days later

'Have you heard yet what Mrs Danforth and the other members of the company plan to do?' de Silva asked Jane.

'She says she'll go back to England. I'm not sure about the rest, apart from Emerald who's staying here.'

'Oh?'

'You aren't really surprised, are you? I'm certainly not. I'd put money on it that we'll have an announcement in a few months' time.'

'Miss Watson and David Hebden?'

'Yes, and I'm sure they'll be very happy.'

'I must say, I hadn't thought of her as a provincial doctor's wife – it's a world away from a travelling life on the stage.'

'That's true, but it's clear she's in love and, given time, people usually adapt. She's such a charming young lady. She'll be a great asset to Nuala.'

He grinned. 'Is this the wisdom of Mrs Appleby or Mrs de Silva?'

'Both.'

He shifted in his chair and let out a yelp. Frowning, Jane reached to pat his uninjured arm. 'Try not to move around too much, dear.'

'I'm trying but I forget.'

'Oh, talking of forgetting, a parcel came for you.' She levered herself out of her seat. 'It's in the hall. I'll fetch it.'

While she was gone, he surveyed the garden. Meringues of cloud drifted across the blue sky and a breeze as light as a cream puff cooled him. Hidden among the trees, a golden oriole sang. There were far worse places to recuperate and, in truth, he was rather looking forward to a respite from police work. It would do Prasanna good to be in charge for a while and Nadar was shaping up. I'm not far away if they need me, he thought, drifting into a doze.

'Here it is.' Jane returned with a neatly wrapped parcel the size of a small brick. 'I'm sorry it took me so long to find it. One of the servants had moved it. You weren't expecting anything, were you? I wonder what it can be.'

'Only one way to find out.'

He reached for the parcel then winced. 'Ouch! You'll have to do it for me.'

Jane shook the parcel. 'It doesn't rattle, and it's quite heavy.'

'Don't keep me in suspense.'

'Patience, dear,' said Jane, undoing the string and taking off the brown paper to reveal a fat book bound in burgundy leather with gold tooling on the spine. She held it up. 'Alexandre Dumas: *The Three Musketeers*. There's a note too. Shall I read it to you?'

'Please.'

To Inspector Shanti de Silva, (Nuala's fifth musketeer!), I hope that you will accept this token of admiration and gratitude from myself and Angel. With best wishes for a speedy recovery, Florence Clutterbuck.

'Gracious! I wasn't expecting that.' Jane giggled. 'I shall have to keep an eye on you and Florence in future.'

De Silva winced, partly from the very idea and partly from the pain that still afflicted his arm.

'Good old Florence. You know perfectly well that won't be necessary. I wonder if she thinks that my part in the sword fight was more swashbuckling than it really was.

Fighting with a cushion and a Roman bust might be a bit of a disappointment.'

'I'm not going to disillusion her,' said Jane with a smile.

He chuckled. 'No, I do rather fancy a moment of glory. Anyway, it was a very kind thought and an amusing choice. I must thank her. Who knows, I might even pick up a few tips.'

Jane smiled. 'Possibly, dear, but I sincerely hope we never have another situation where you need to use them. Now, I have things to see to. Will you be alright on your own for a while?'

'Of course.'

'Shall I put on some music for you?'

'That would be nice.'

'Anything in particular?'

'No, you choose.'

As Jane disappeared into the house, his thoughts turned to Frank Sheridan. The actor had often been on de Silva's mind in the last few days. The charitable view was that Sheridan had been almost as much a victim as Alexander Danforth. One could see him as the helpless pawn of his condition: two men trapped in one body. Jane said it reminded her of the story of Dr Jekyll and Mr Hyde.

De Silva wondered, not for the first time, why Sheridan had written those words on the mirror: *the rest is silence*. Unless Danforth had let something slip, Sheridan was very unlikely to have known that Polly Devlin had died. But he clearly bore Danforth a grudge that went beyond rational bounds for depriving him of the woman he loved. In Sheridan's twisted state of mind, were those words his marker that he had finally exacted revenge on the friend who, in his dark hours, he regarded as his worst enemy?

The soothing strains of a Chopin *Nocturne* drifted from the house. De Silva decided to put unanswerable questions aside. If he was honest, although he had no need of silence, a rest was very welcome.

He opened *The Three Musketeers* and settled down to read.

HISTORICAL NOTE

The abdication of Edward VIII is touched on in this book and some further explanation may be of interest to readers.

In our present age of instant global communication and social media, it's hard to credit that the British public was largely unaware of the crisis that loomed for the monarchy in 1936. It was the case, however, although the story was being widely reported abroad, especially in the American press. The King's insistence on marrying the twice-divorced American socialite, Wallis Simpson, with whom he had been having an affair for several years, rocked the throne. His ministers and the Church of England, of which he was head, were violently opposed to the match.

It wasn't until early December that the British press broke their silence when they took a remark by the Bishop of Bradford about the King's need for spiritual guidance as licence to print. On December 11th, the Abdication Bill passed into law and Edward and Mrs Simpson left for France. His brother, George, who suffered from shyness and a terrible stammer, reluctantly succeeded him as George VI.

Made in the USA
Middletown, DE
11 March 2018